FAR OUT FABLES

STONE ARCH BOOKS
a capstone imprint

INTRODUCING...

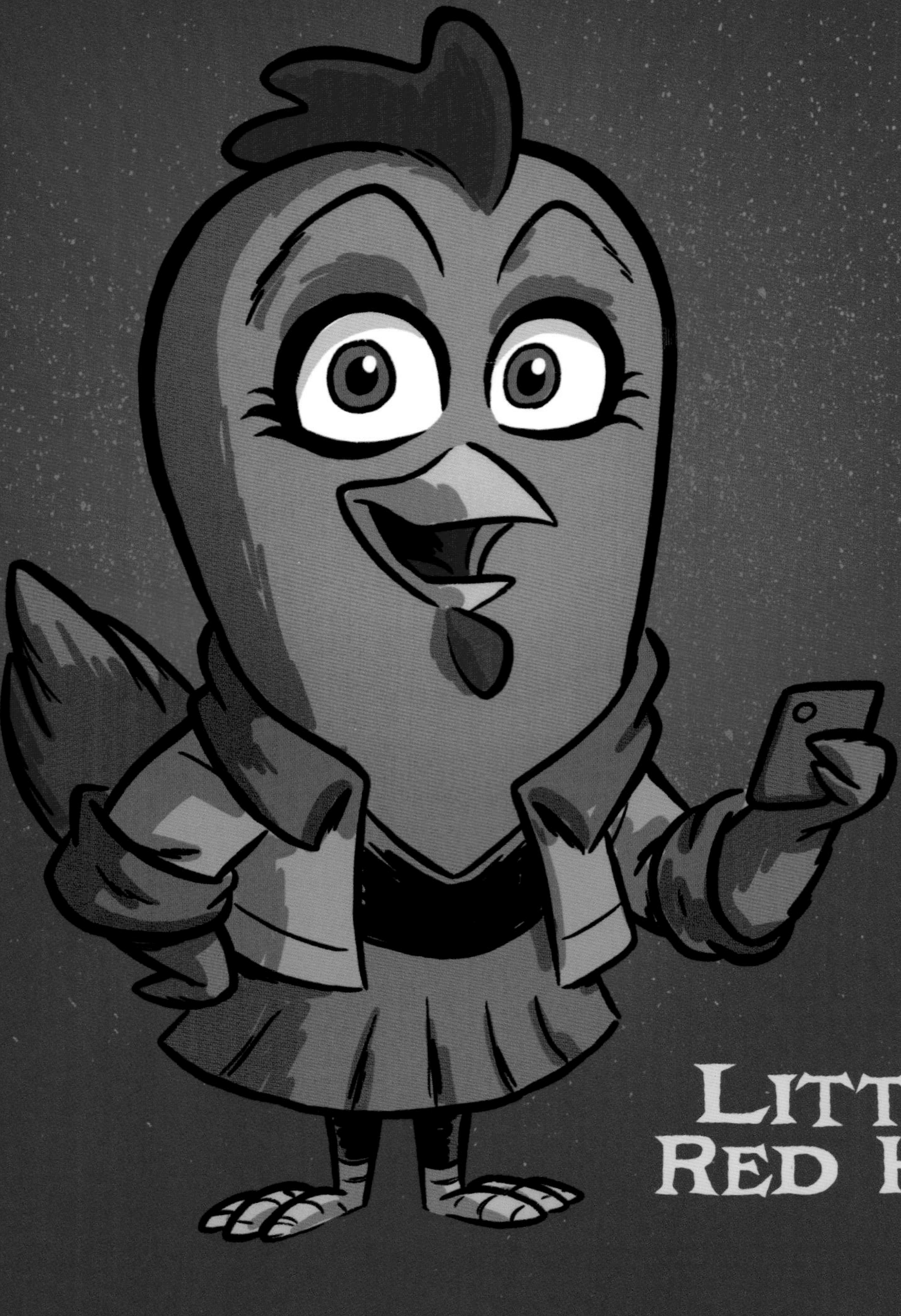

LITTLE RED HEN

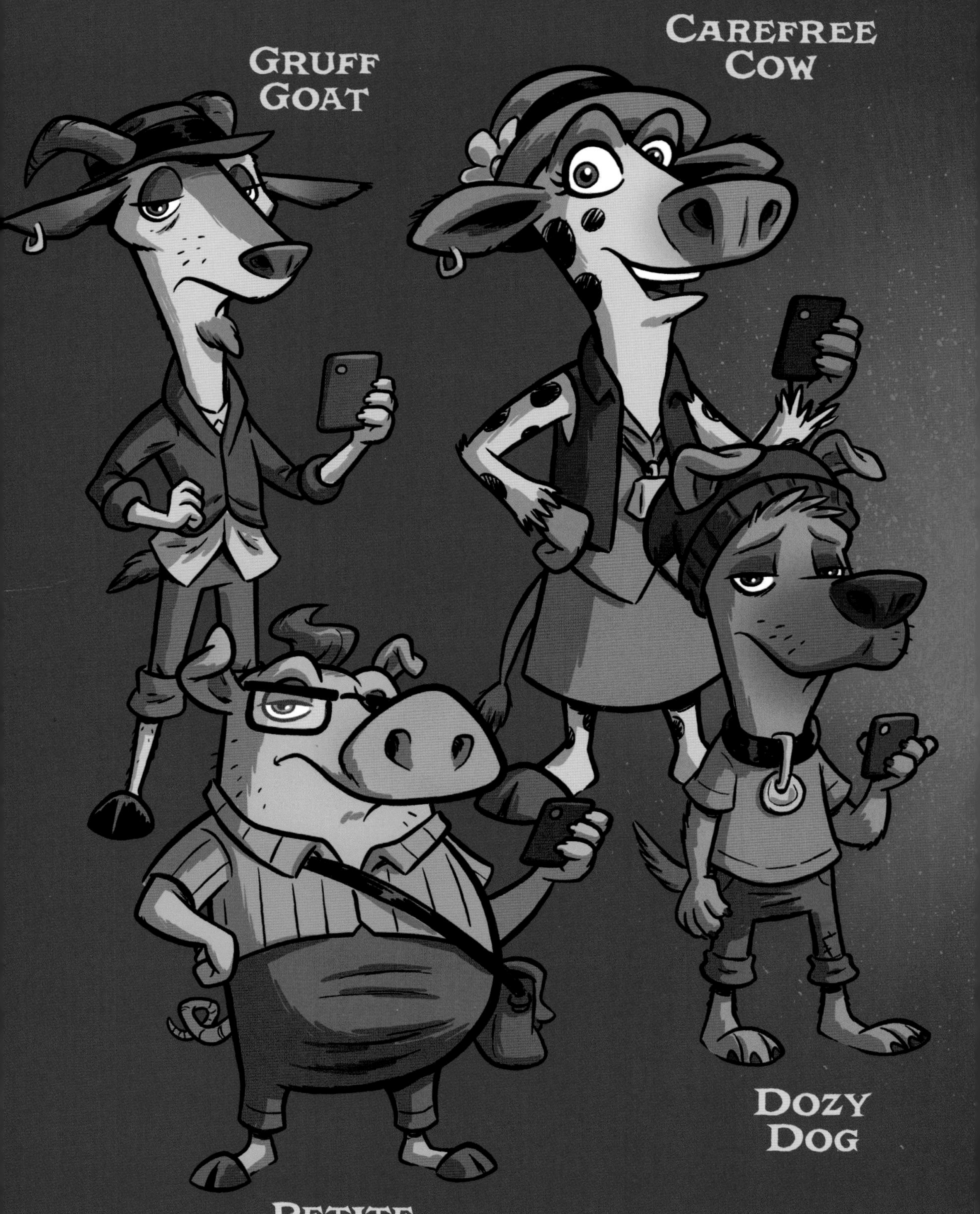
GRUFF GOAT
CAREFREE COW
PETITE PIG
DOZY DOG

IN...

Far Out Fables is published by
Stone Arch Books,
an imprint of Capstone.
1710 Roe Crest Drive
North Mankato, Minnesota 56003
www.capstonepub.com

Cataloging-in-Publication Data is
available on the Library of Congress
website.

ISBN: 978-1-5158-8220-6 (hardcover)
ISBN: 978-1-5158-8329-6 (paperback)
ISBN: 978-1-5158-9207-6 (eBook PDF)

Summary: Other animals in Barnyard
Meadows are online all day, but
Little Red Hen wants to actually
make something. So she's creating
an internet baking show! But with
her friends unwilling to do any work
and each step of the process filled
with unusual challenges, can Red push
through to become a video star?

Designer: Hilary Wacholz
Editor: Abby Huff
Letterer: Jaymes Reed

Printed and bound in China.   PO4205

FAR OUT FABLES

LITTLE RED HEN, VIDEO STAR

A GRAPHIC NOVEL

BY STEVE FOXE

ILLUSTRATED BY OTIS FRAMPTON

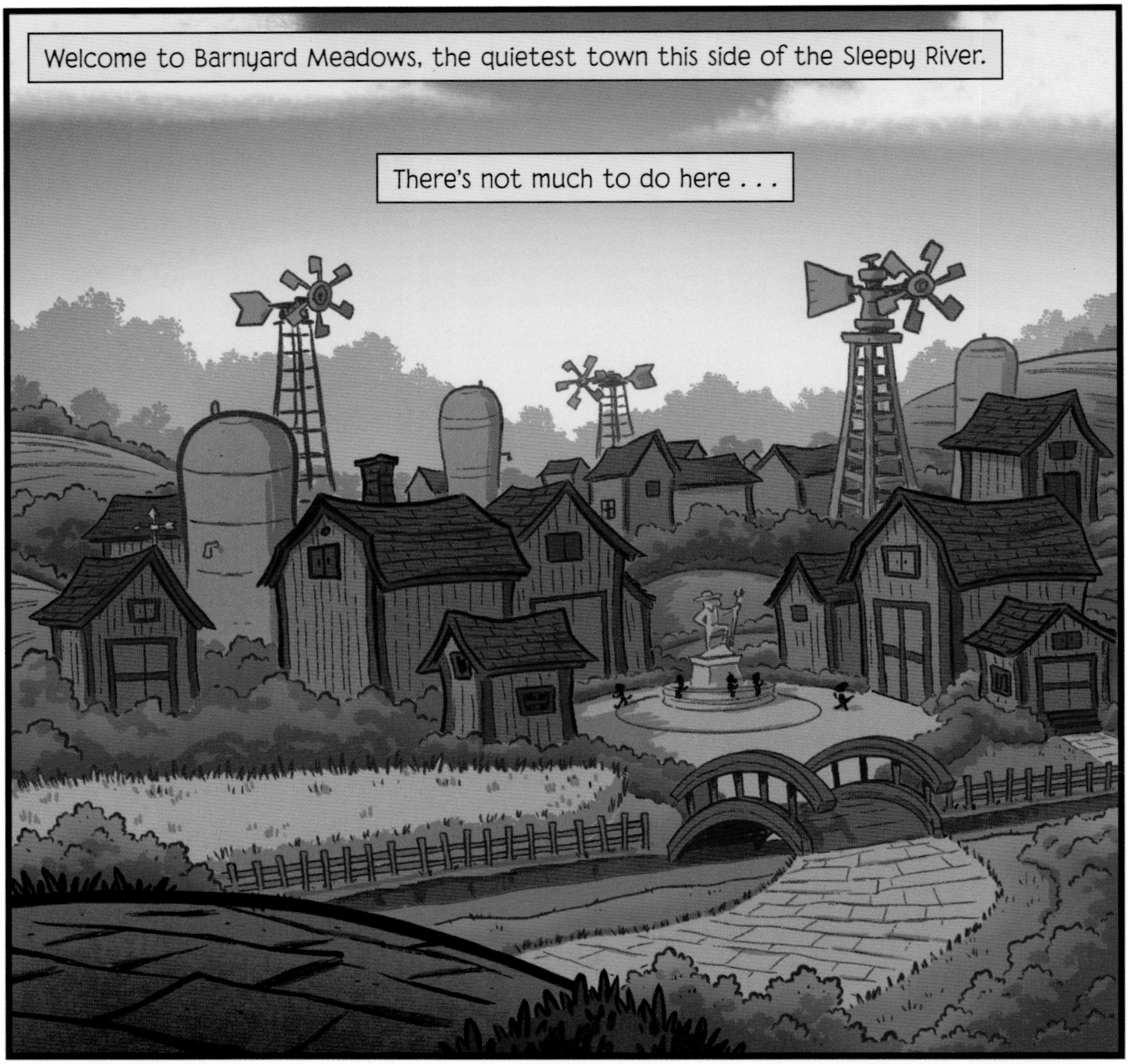
Welcome to Barnyard Meadows, the quietest town this side of the Sleepy River.
There's not much to do here . . .

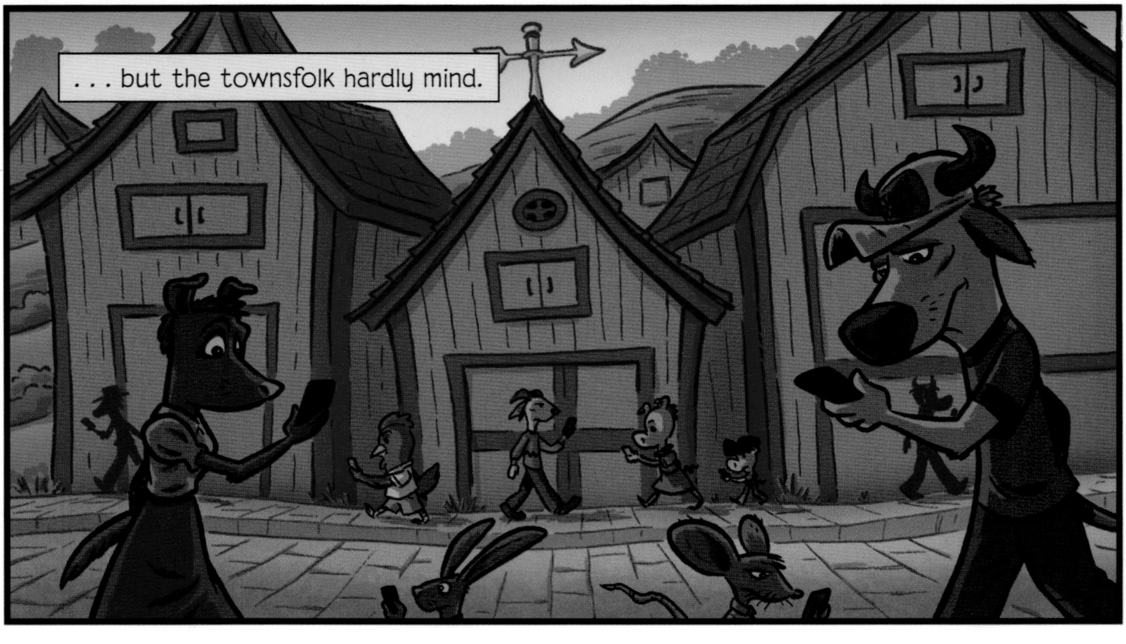
. . . but the townsfolk hardly mind.

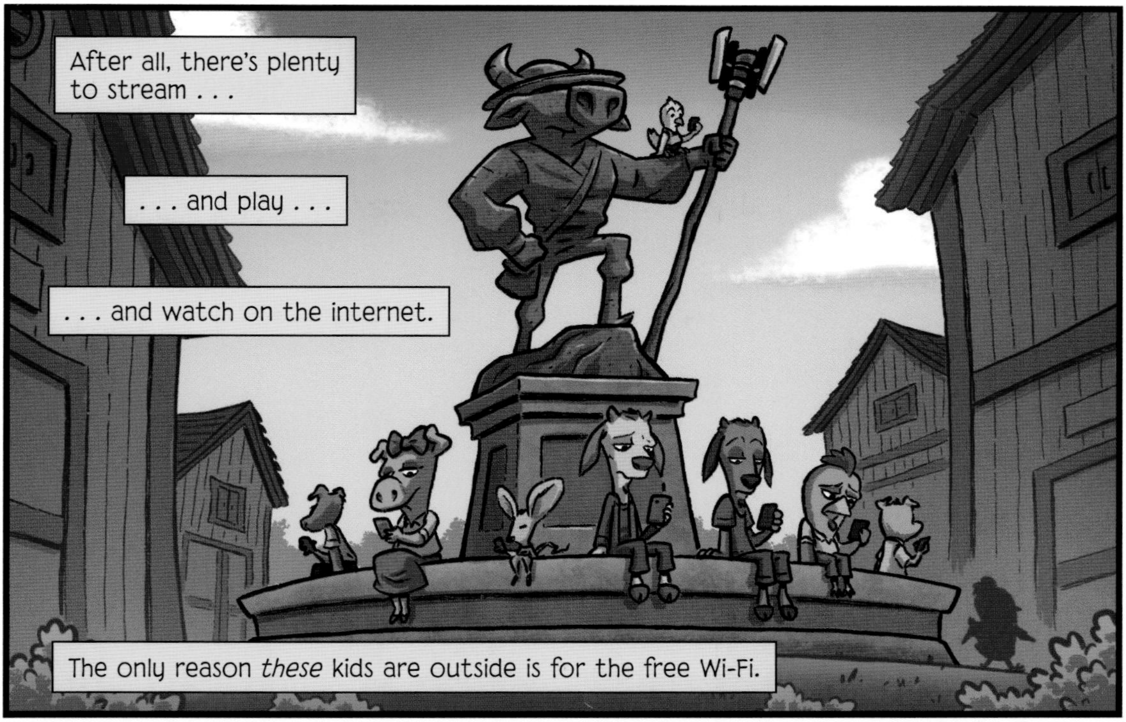
After all, there's plenty to stream . . .
. . . and play . . .
. . . and watch on the internet.
The only reason *these* kids are outside is for the free Wi-Fi.

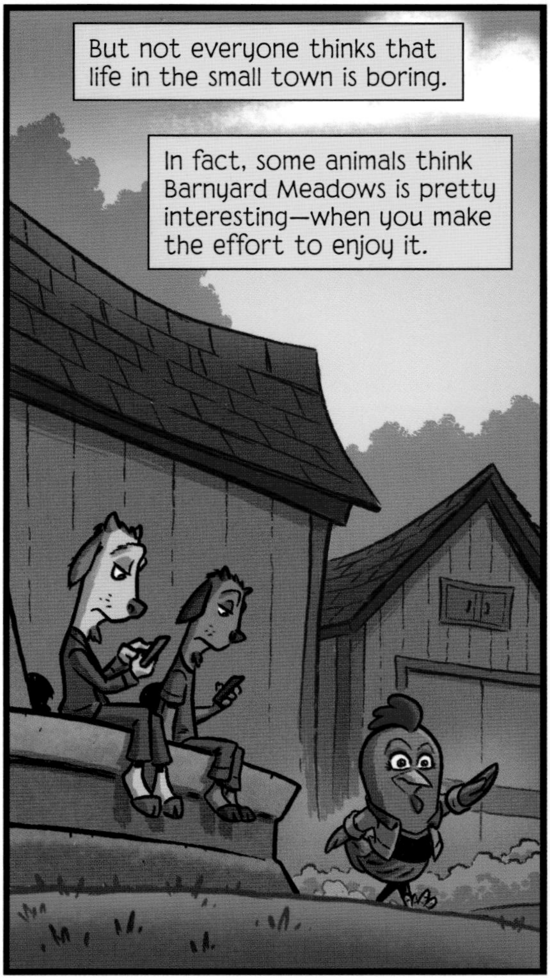
But not everyone thinks that life in the small town is boring.
In fact, some animals think Barnyard Meadows is pretty interesting—when you make the effort to enjoy it.

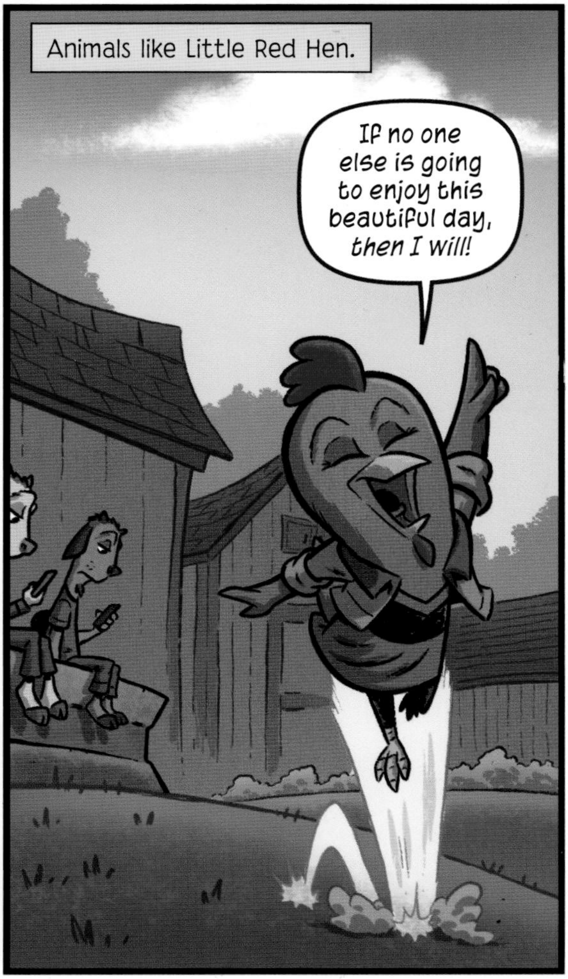
Animals like Little Red Hen.
If no one else is going to enjoy this beautiful day, *then I will!*

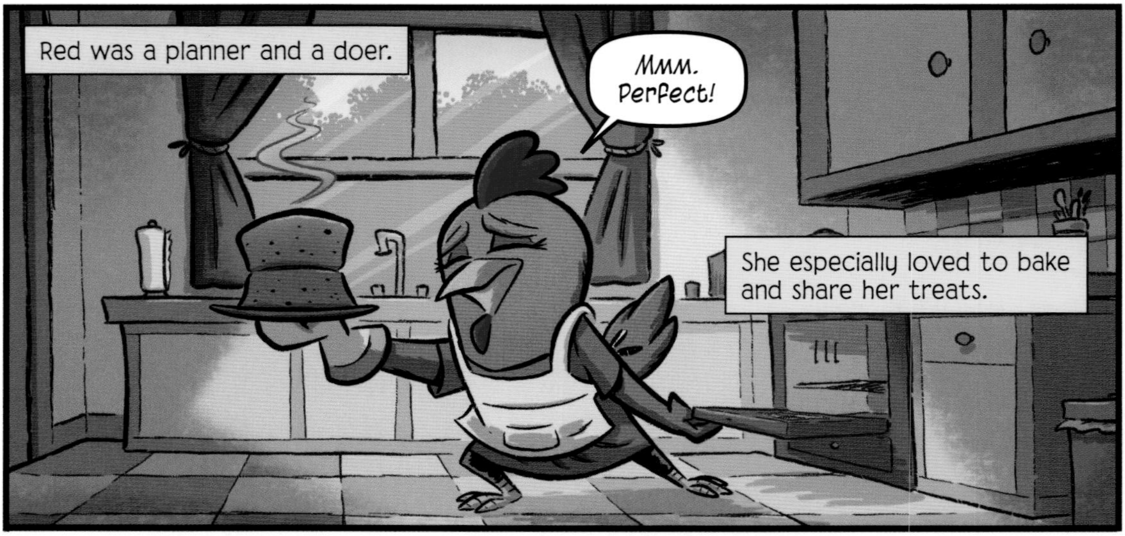
Red was a planner and a doer.
MMM. Perfect!
She especially loved to bake and share her treats.

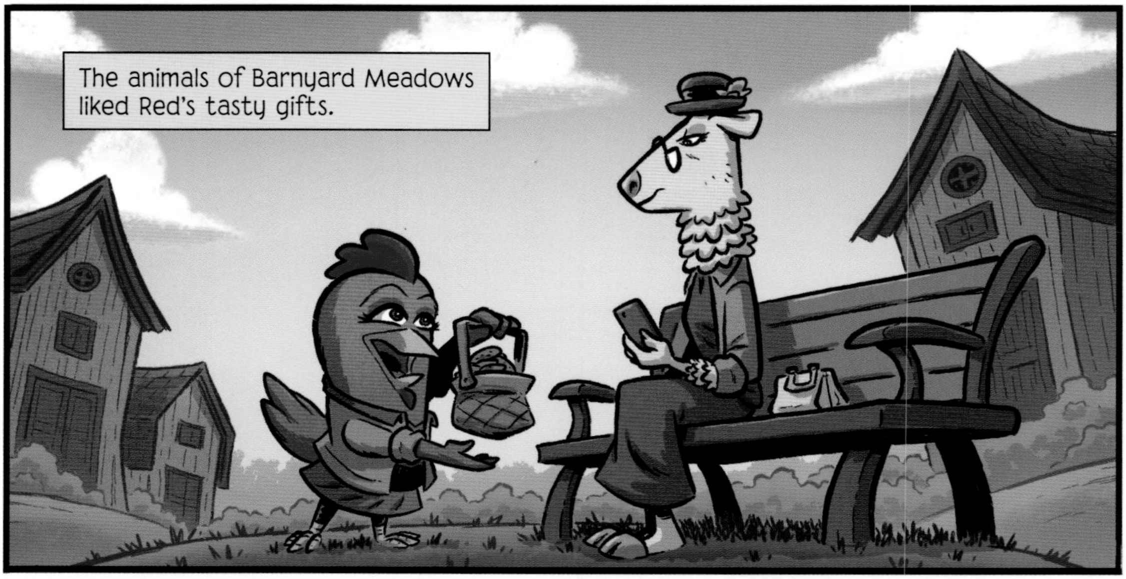
The animals of Barnyard Meadows liked Red's tasty gifts.

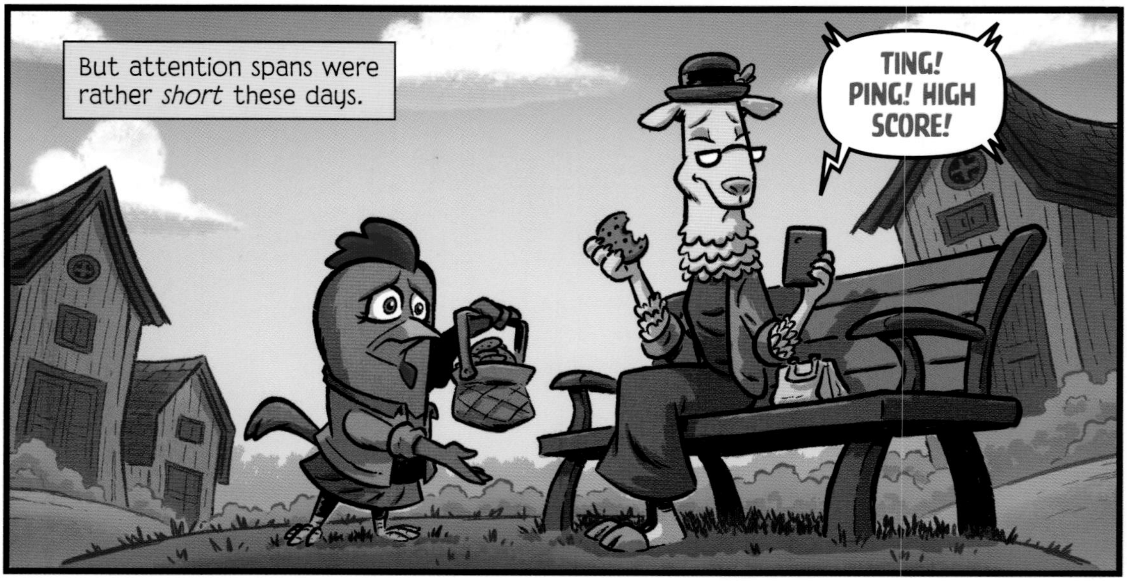
But attention spans were rather *short* these days.
TING! PING! HIGH SCORE!

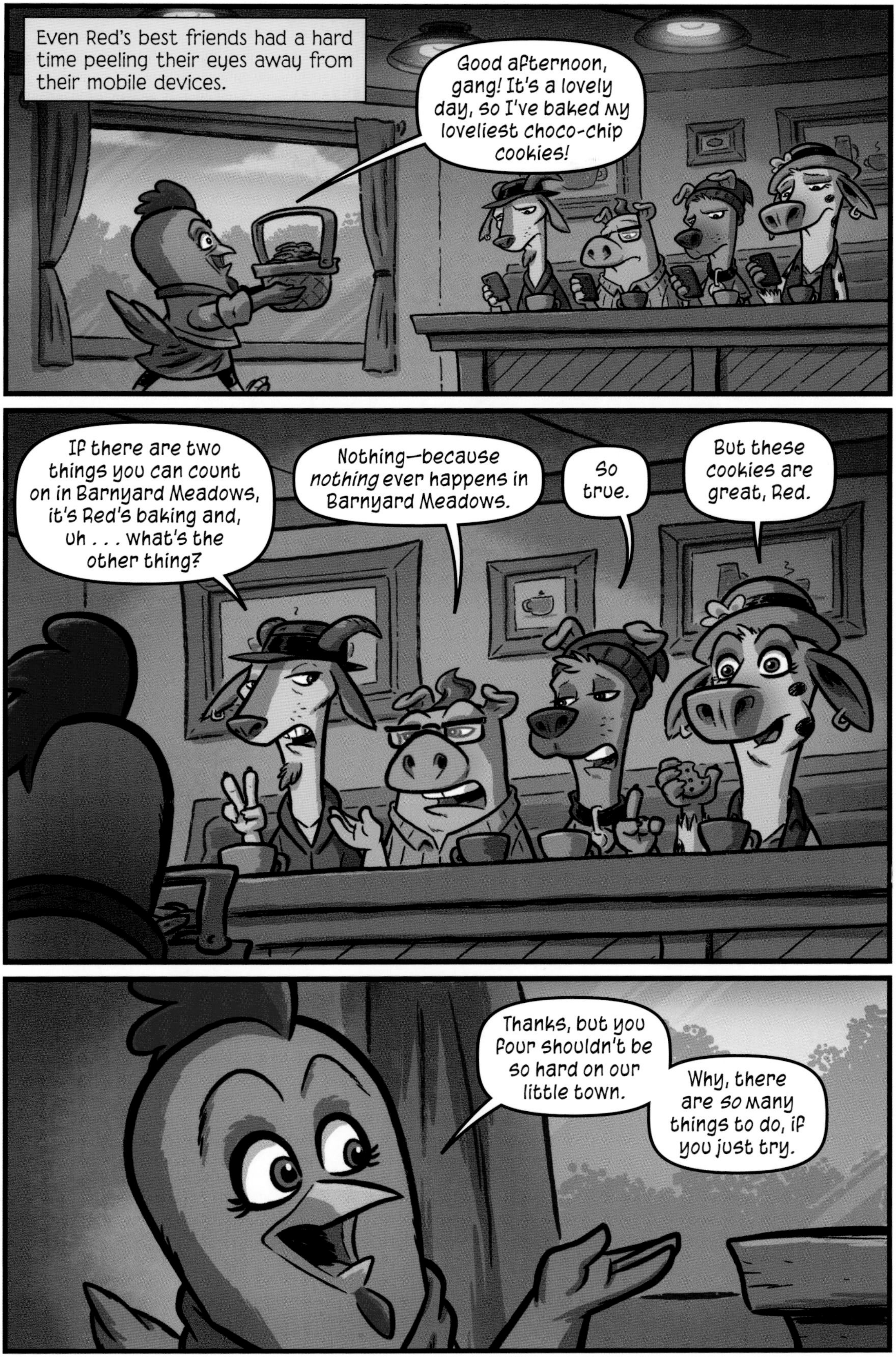
Even Red's best friends had a hard time peeling their eyes away from their mobile devices.
Good afternoon, gang! It's a lovely day, so I've baked my loveliest choco-chip cookies!
If there are two things you can count on in Barnyard Meadows, it's Red's baking and, uh . . . what's the other thing?
Nothing—because *nothing* ever happens in Barnyard Meadows.
So true.
But these cookies are great, Red.
Thanks, but you four shouldn't be so hard on our little town.
Why, there are *so* many things to do, if you just try.

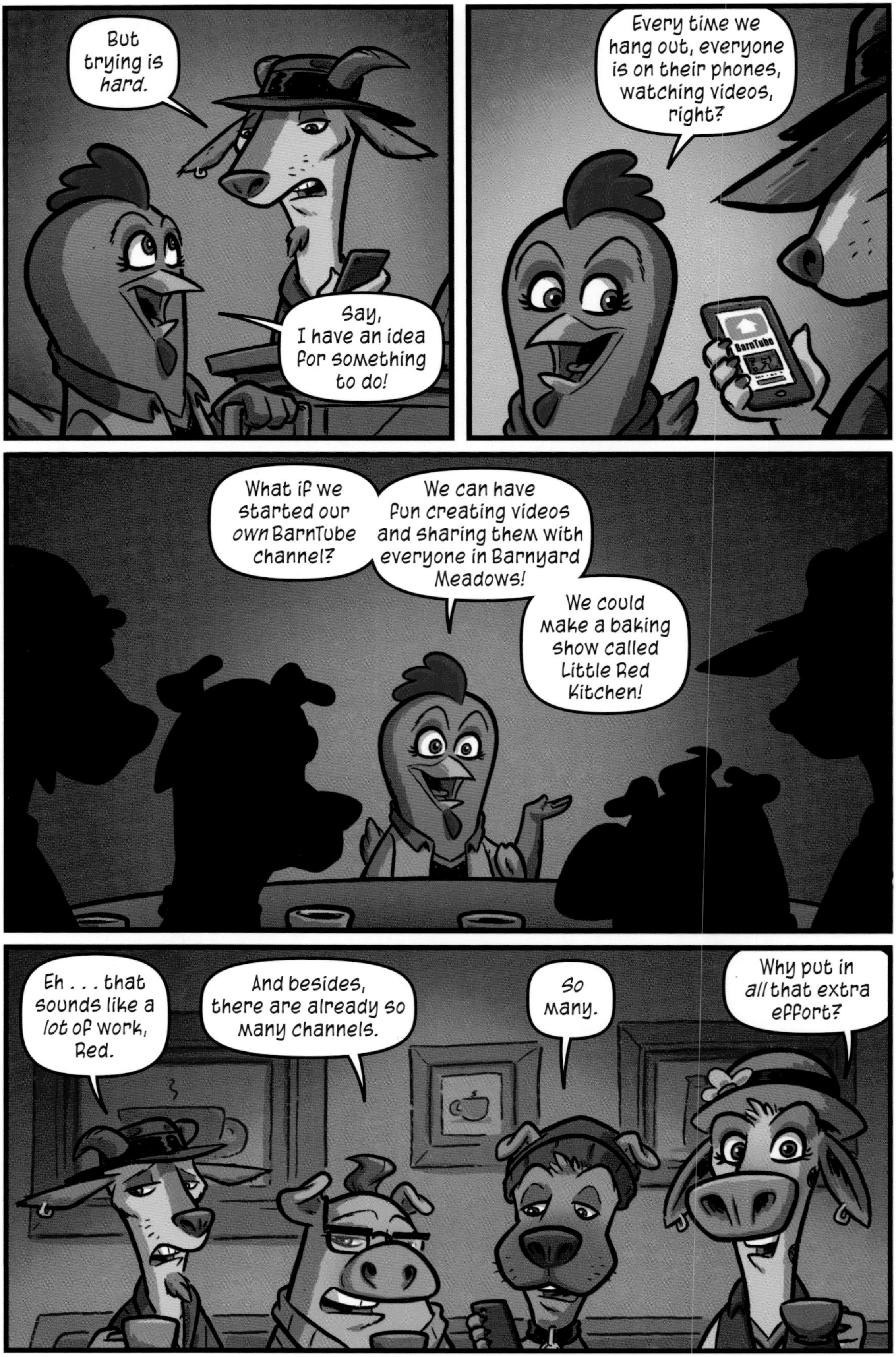
But trying is hard.
Say, I have an idea for something to do!
Every time we hang out, everyone is on their phones, watching videos, right?
BarnTube
What if we started our own BarnTube channel?
We can have fun creating videos and sharing them with everyone in Barnyard Meadows!
We could make a baking show called Little Red Kitchen!
Eh . . . that sounds like a lot of work, Red.
And besides, there are already so many channels.
So many.
Why put in all that extra effort?

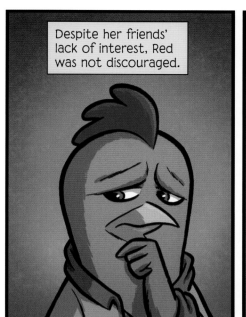

Despite her friends' lack of interest, Red was not discouraged.

Well, maybe she was a little bit . . .

But only for a moment.

You just need to see things in action. Then you'll be *totally* into the idea.

If you don't want to work on the channel right now, then I will!

Thanks for your feedback!

CAFÉ

That was awkward.

11

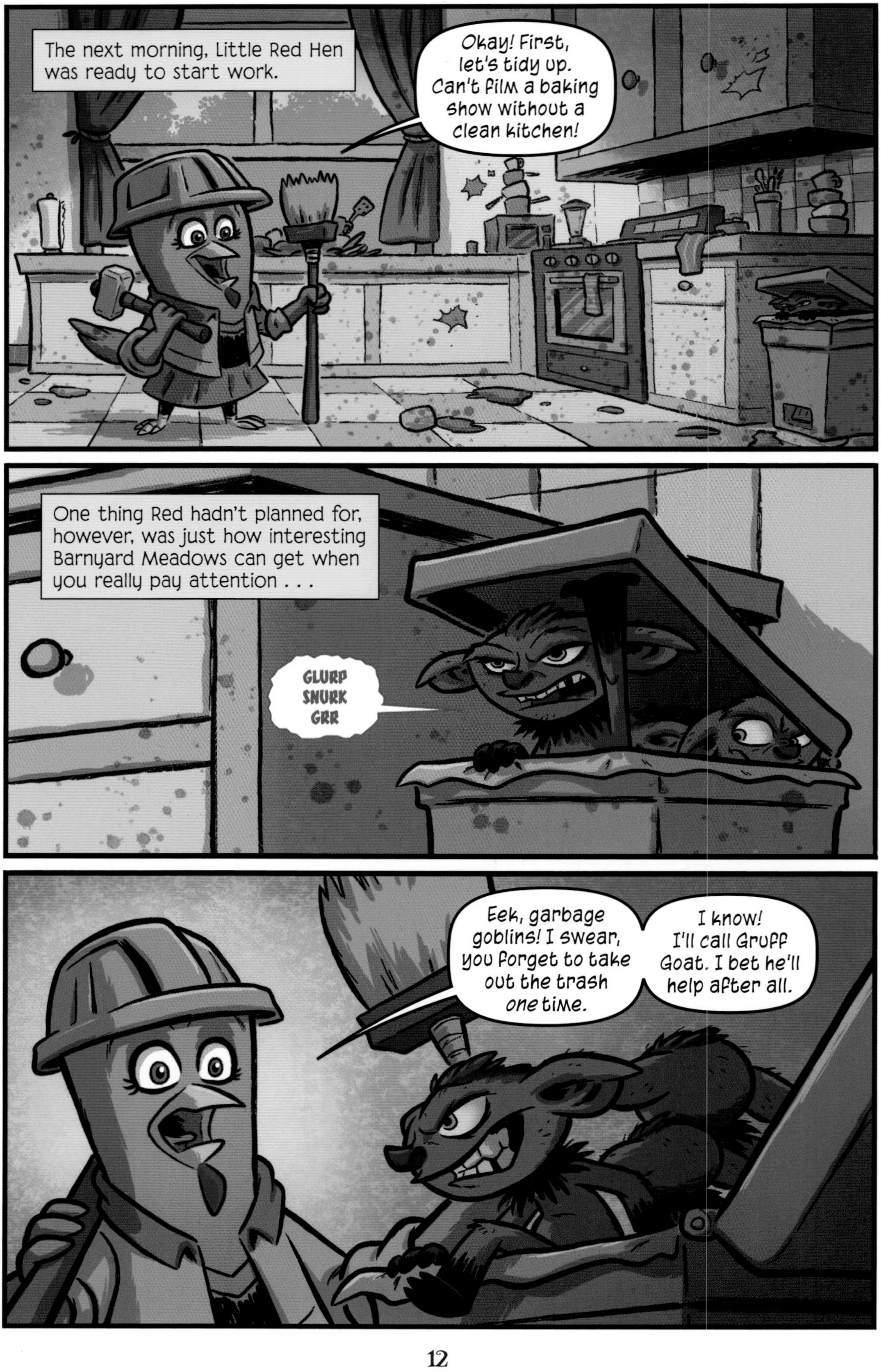
The next morning, Little Red Hen was ready to start work.
Okay! First, let's tidy up. Can't film a baking show without a clean kitchen!
One thing Red hadn't planned for, however, was just how interesting Barnyard Meadows can get when you really pay attention . . .
GLURP SNURK GRR
Eek, garbage goblins! I swear, you forget to take out the trash *one* time.
I know! I'll call Gruff Goat. I bet he'll help after all.

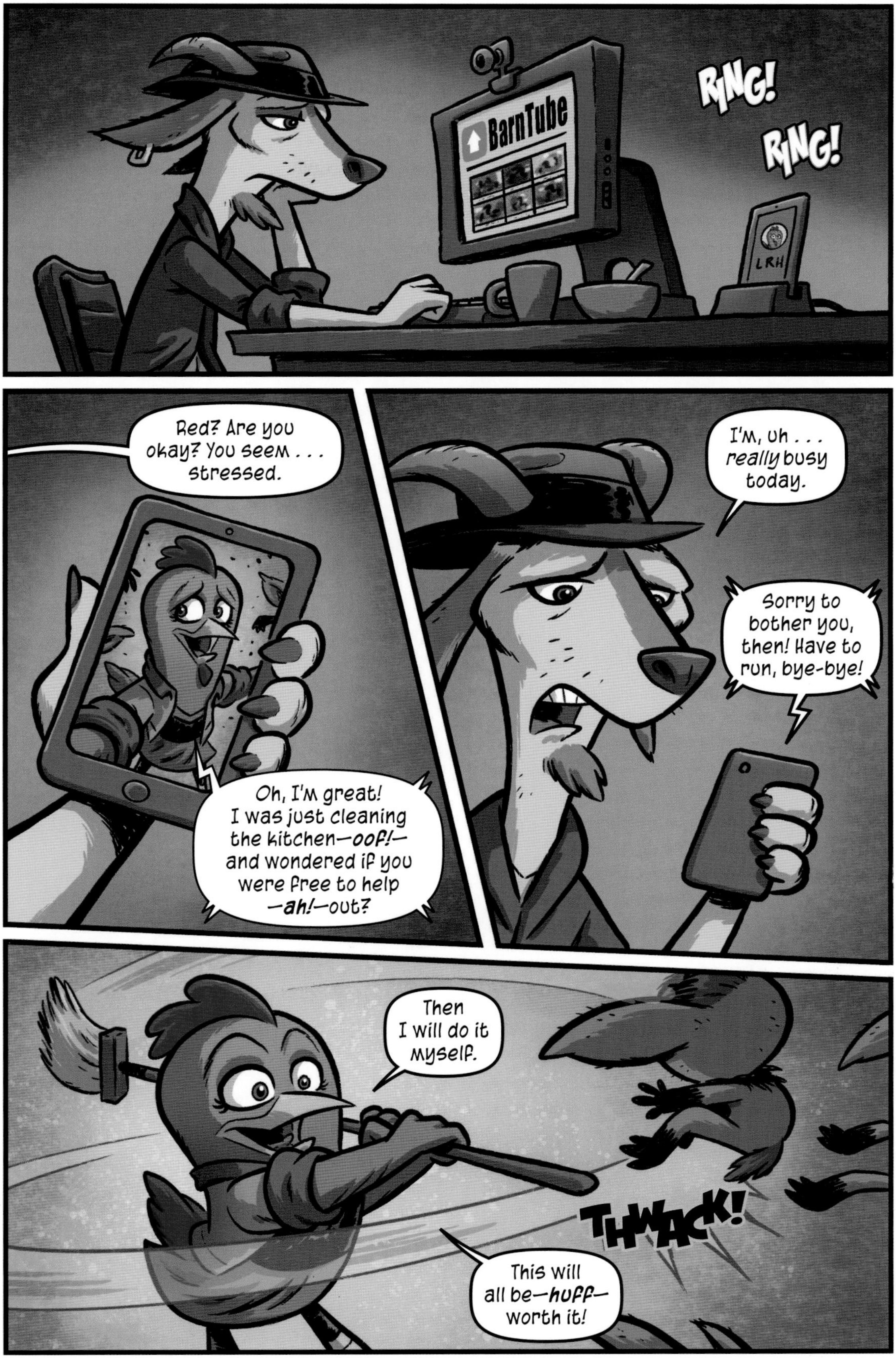
RING!
RING!
BarnTube
LRH
Red? Are you okay? You seem . . . stressed.
Oh, I'm great! I was just cleaning the kitchen—oof!—and wondered if you were free to help —ah!—out?
I'm, uh . . . really busy today.
Sorry to bother you, then! Have to run, bye-bye!
Then I will do it myself.
THWACK!
This will all be—huff—worth it!

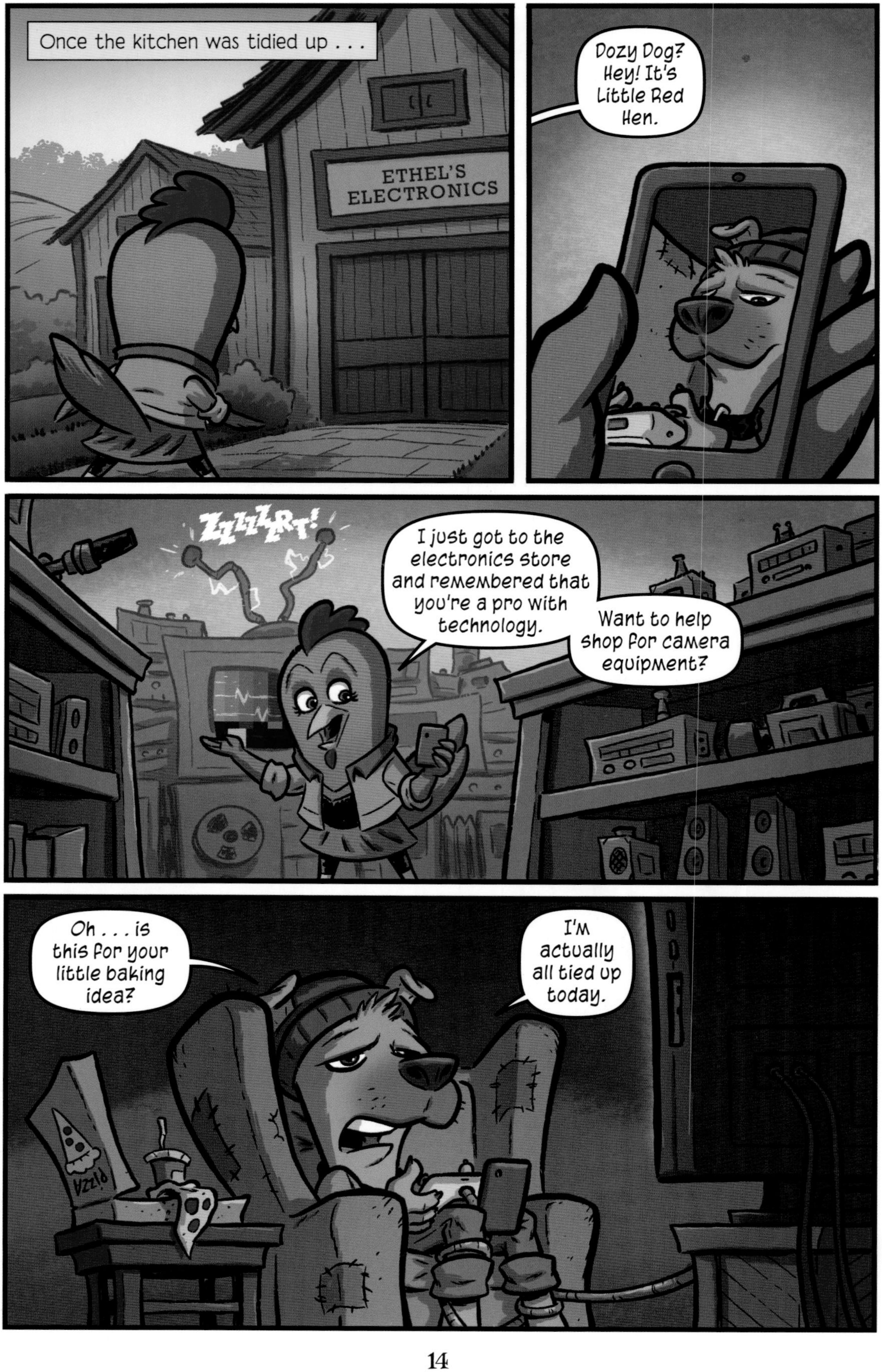
Once the kitchen was tidied up . . .
ETHEL'S ELECTRONICS
Dozy Dog? Hey! It's Little Red Hen.
ZZZZZZRT!
I just got to the electronics store and remembered that you're a pro with technology.
Want to help shop for camera equipment?
Oh . . . is this for your little baking idea?
I'm actually all tied up today.
PIZZA

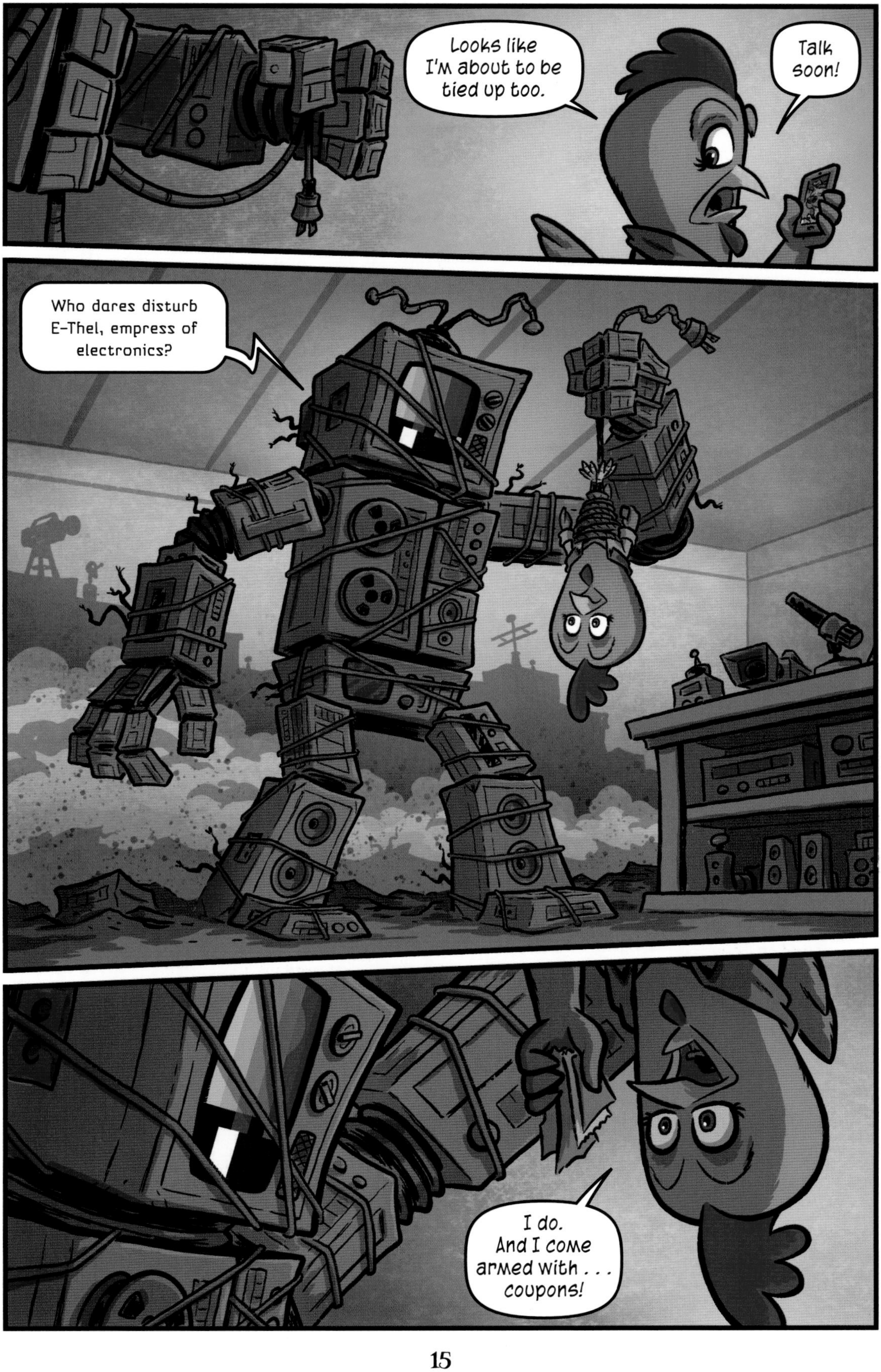
Looks like I'm about to be tied up too.
Talk soon!
Who dares disturb E-Thel, empress of electronics?
I do. And I come armed with . . . coupons!

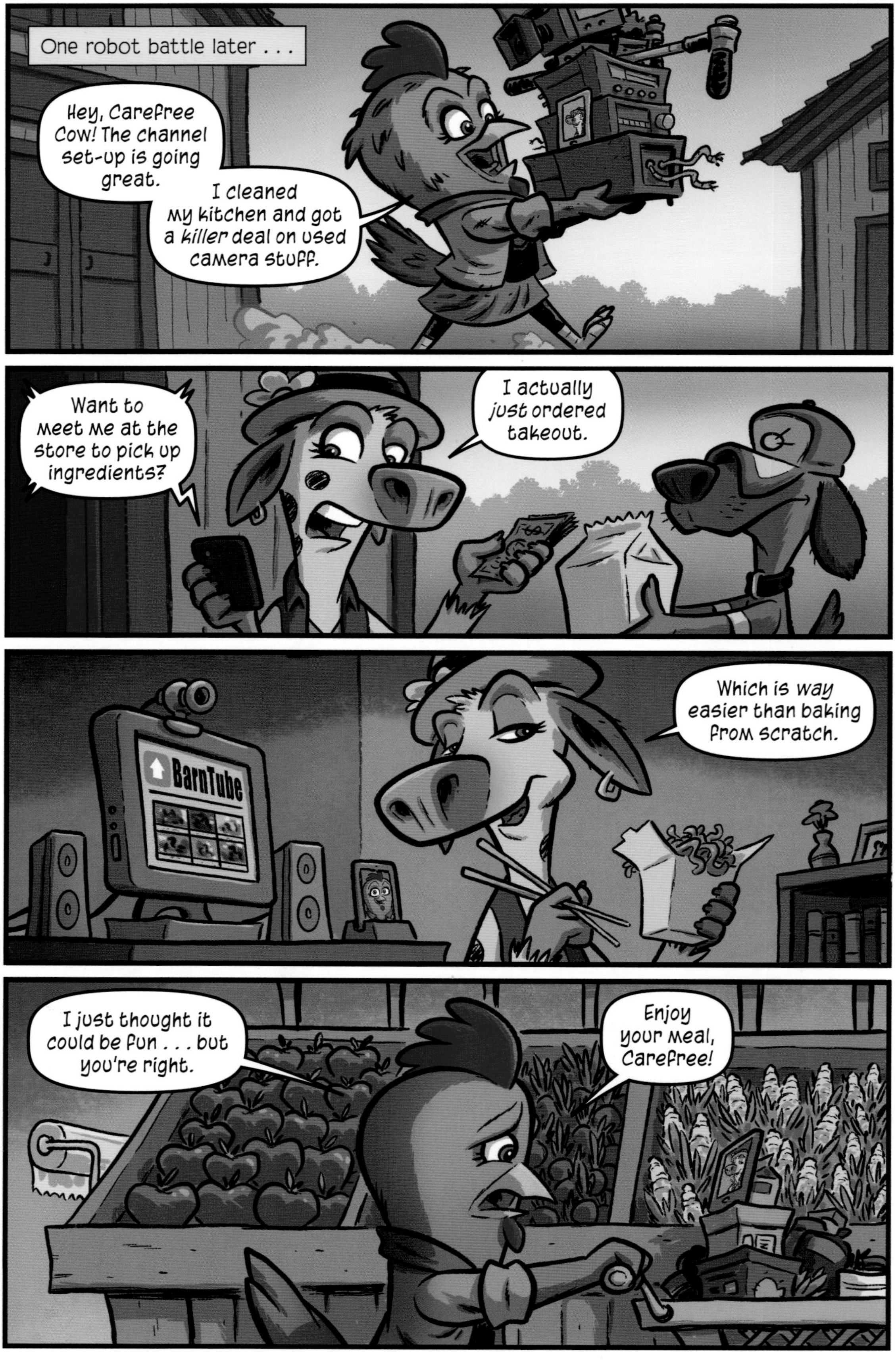
One robot battle later . . .
Hey, Carefree Cow! The channel set-up is going great.
I cleaned my kitchen and got a *killer* deal on used camera stuff.
Want to meet me at the store to pick up ingredients?
I actually *just* ordered takeout.
BarnTube
Which is *way* easier than baking from scratch.
I just thought it could be fun . . . but you're right.
Enjoy your meal, Carefree!

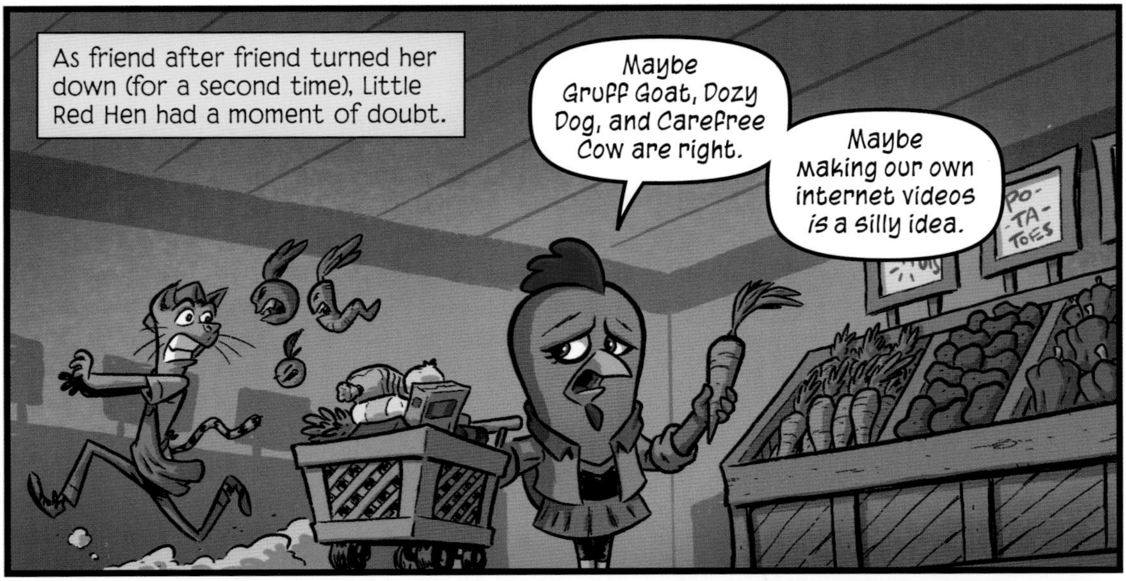
As friend after friend turned her down (for a second time), Little Red Hen had a moment of doubt.
Maybe Gruff Goat, Dozy Dog, and Carefree Cow are right.
Maybe making our own internet videos is a silly idea.
PO- TA- TOES

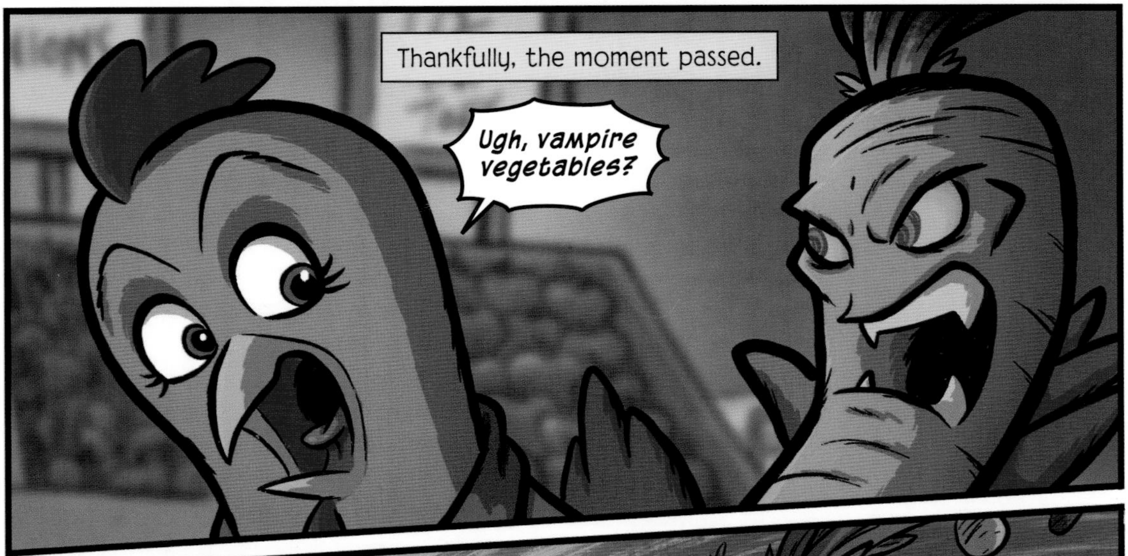
Thankfully, the moment passed.
Ugh, vampire vegetables?

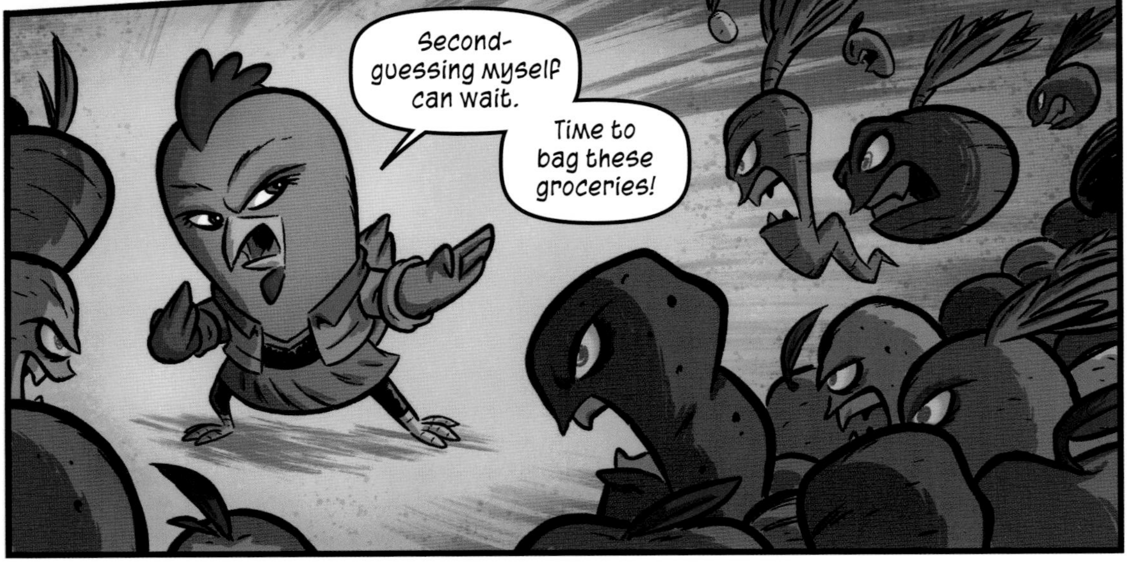
Second-guessing myself can wait.
Time to bag these groceries!

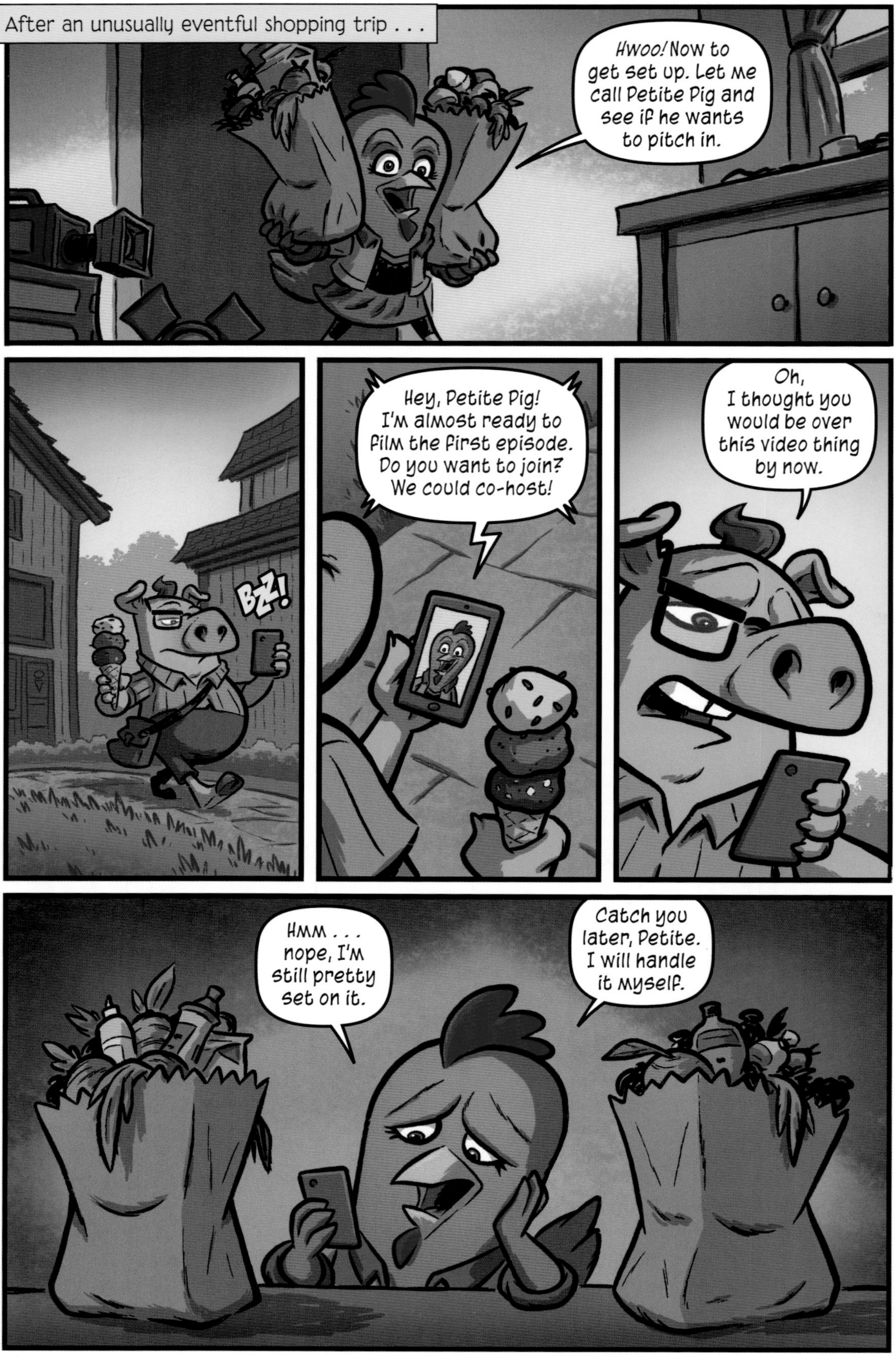
After an unusually eventful shopping trip . . .
Hwoo! Now to get set up. Let me call Petite Pig and see if he wants to pitch in.
BZZ!
Hey, Petite Pig! I'm almost ready to film the first episode. Do you want to join? We could co-host!
Oh, I thought you would be over this video thing by now.
Hmm . . . nope, I'm still pretty set on it.
Catch you later, Petite. I will handle it myself.

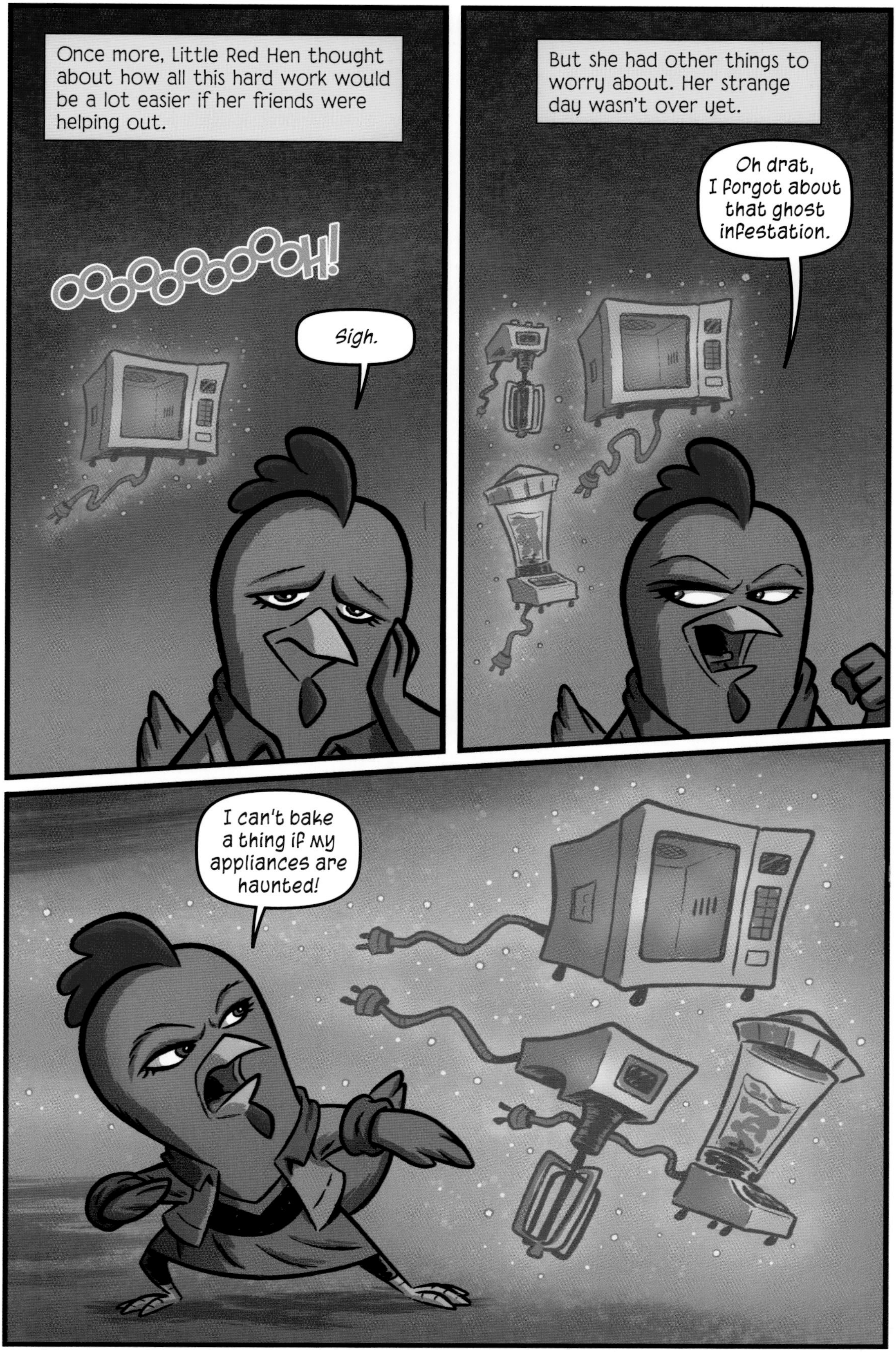
Once more, Little Red Hen thought about how all this hard work would be a lot easier if her friends were helping out.
OOOOOOOOOOH!
Sigh.
But she had other things to worry about. Her strange day wasn't over yet.
Oh drat, I forgot about that ghost infestation.
I can't bake a thing if my appliances are haunted!

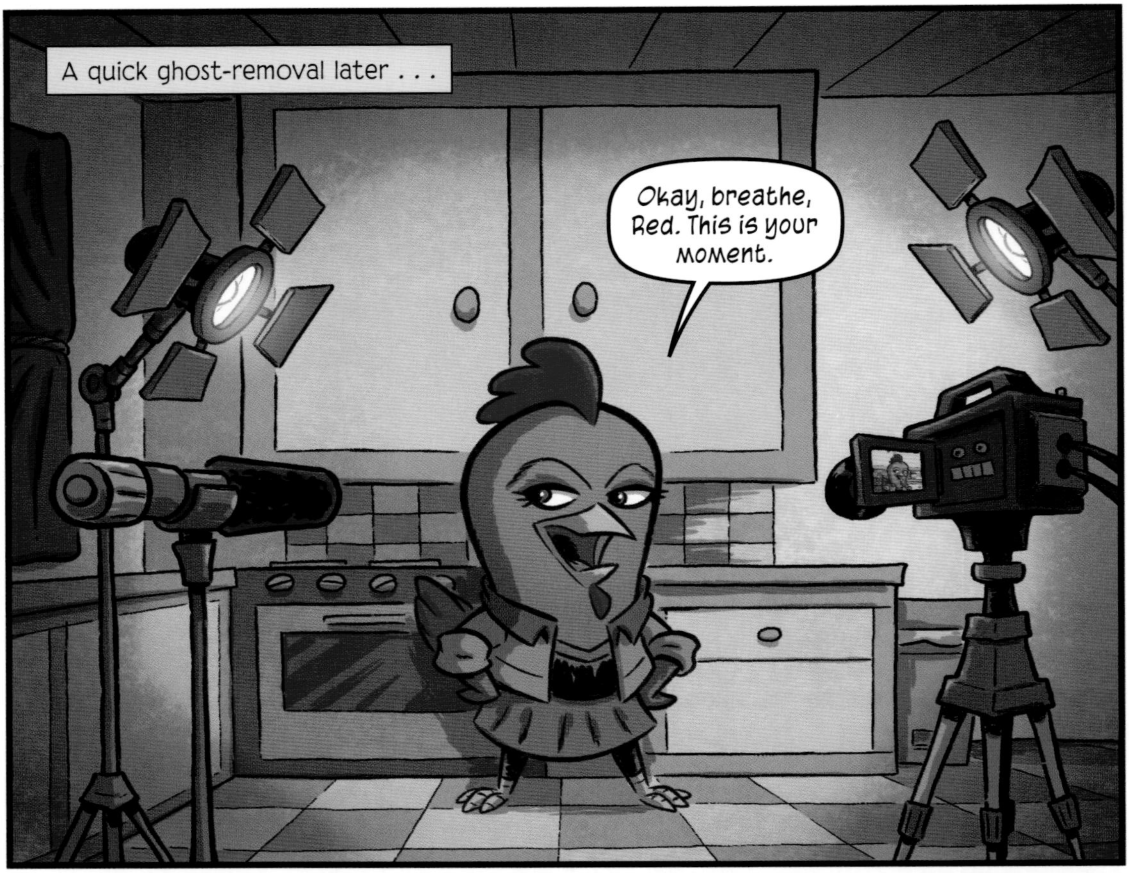
A quick ghost-removal later . . .
Okay, breathe, Red. This is your moment.

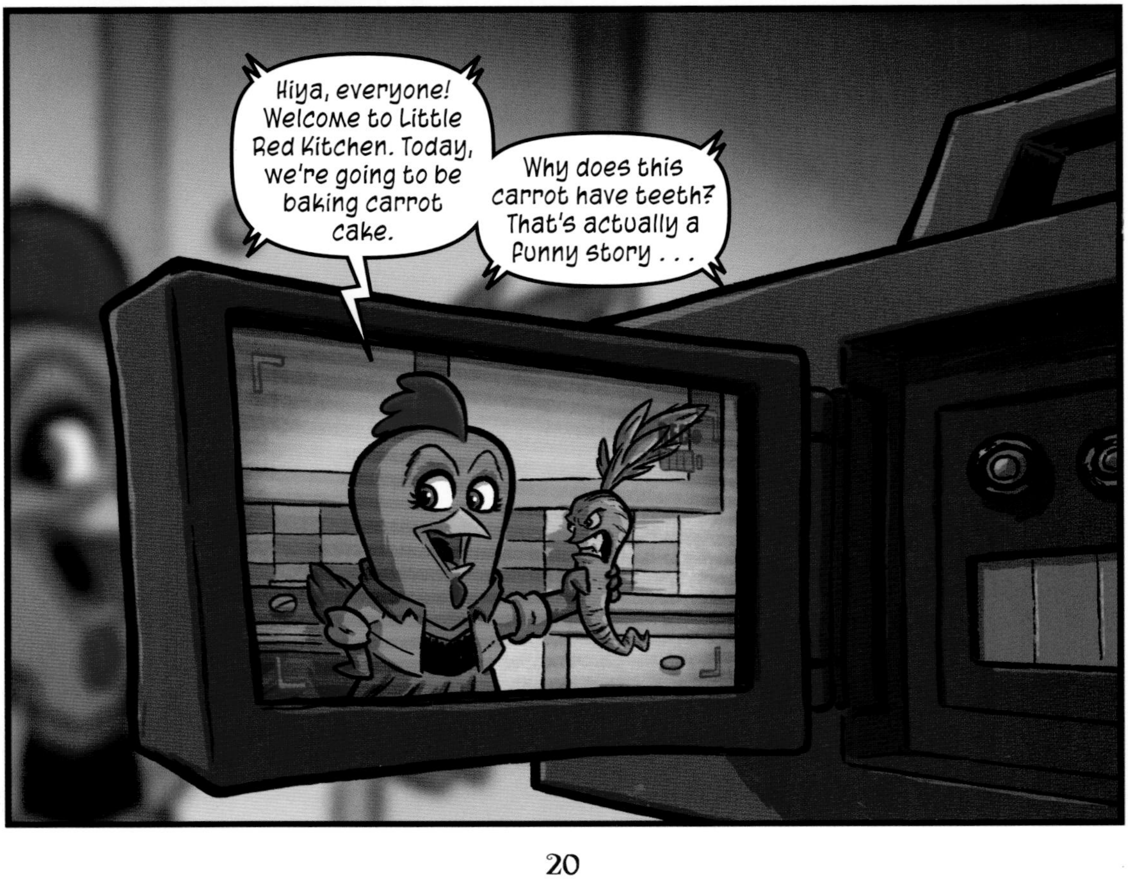
Hiya, everyone! Welcome to Little Red Kitchen. Today, we're going to be baking carrot cake.
Why does this carrot have teeth? That's actually a funny story . . .

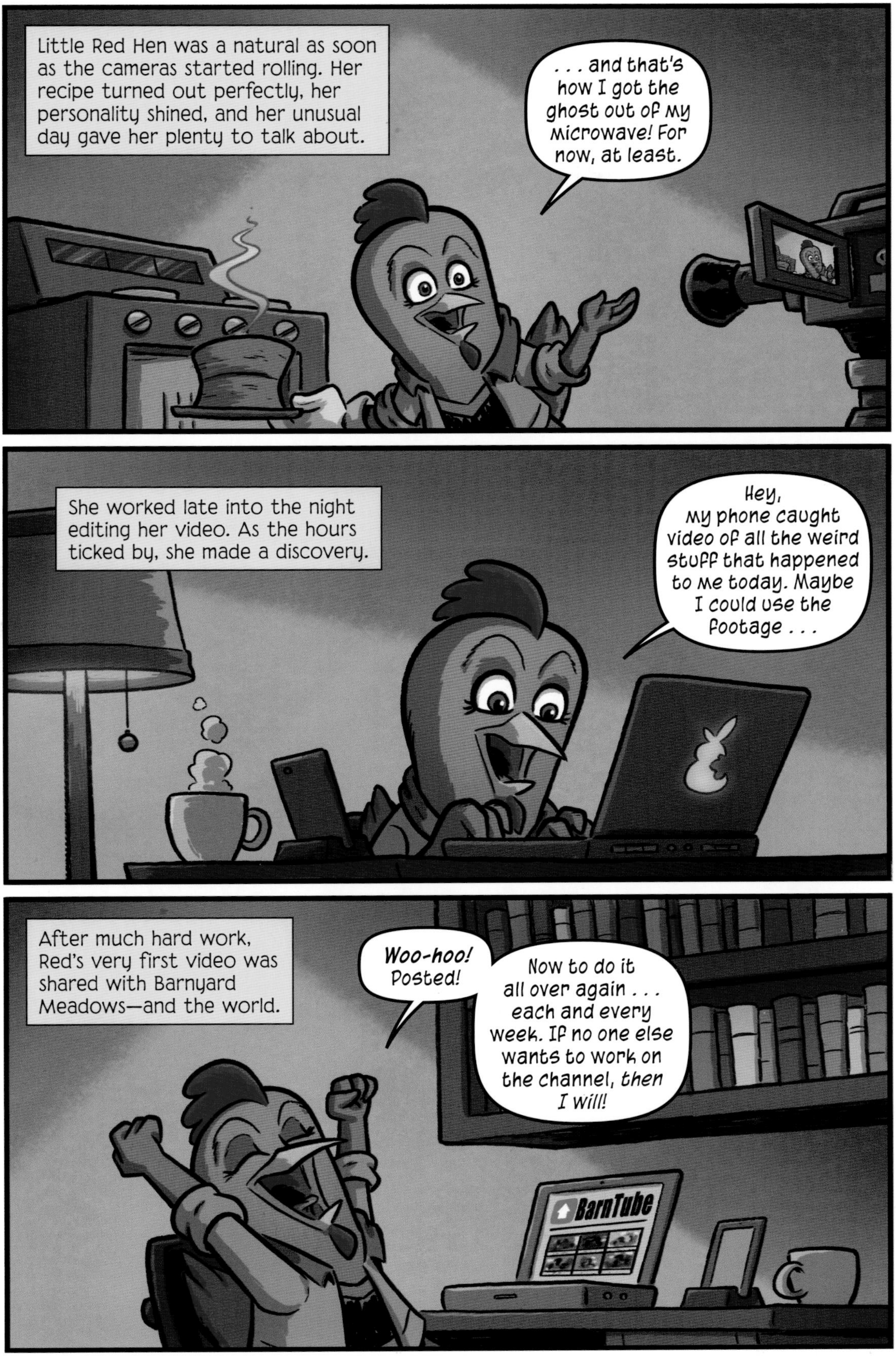
Little Red Hen was a natural as soon as the cameras started rolling. Her recipe turned out perfectly, her personality shined, and her unusual day gave her plenty to talk about.
. . . and that's how I got the ghost out of my microwave! For now, at least.
She worked late into the night editing her video. As the hours ticked by, she made a discovery.
Hey, my phone caught video of all the weird stuff that happened to me today. Maybe I could use the footage . . .
After much hard work, Red's very first video was shared with Barnyard Meadows—and the world.
Woo-hoo! Posted!
Now to do it all over again . . . each and every week. If no one else wants to work on the channel, *then I will!*
BarnTube

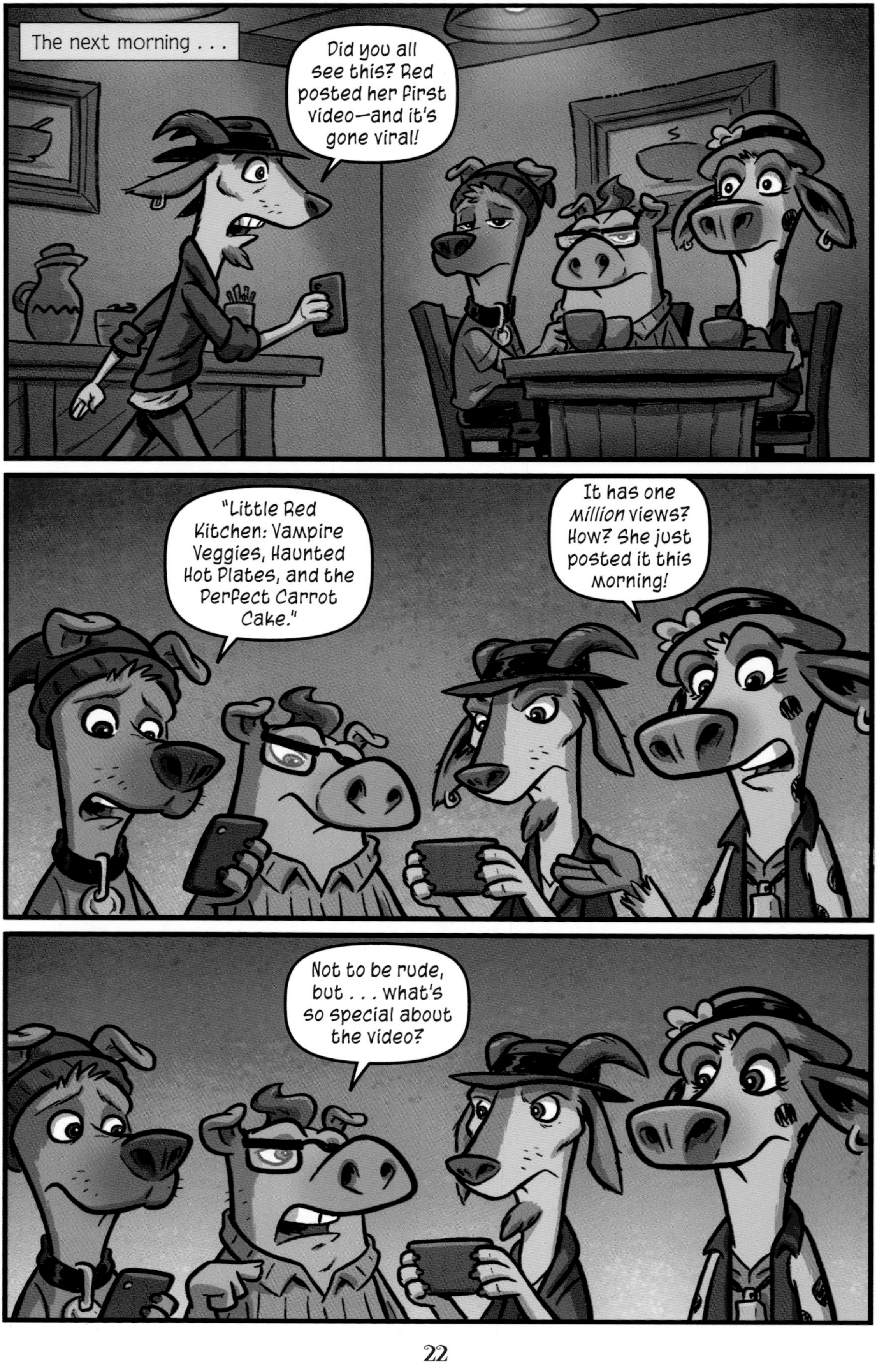
The next morning . . .
Did you all see this? Red posted her first video—and it's gone viral!
"Little Red Kitchen: Vampire Veggies, Haunted Hot Plates, and the Perfect Carrot Cake."
It has one *million* views? How? She just posted it this morning!
Not to be rude, but . . . what's so special about the video?

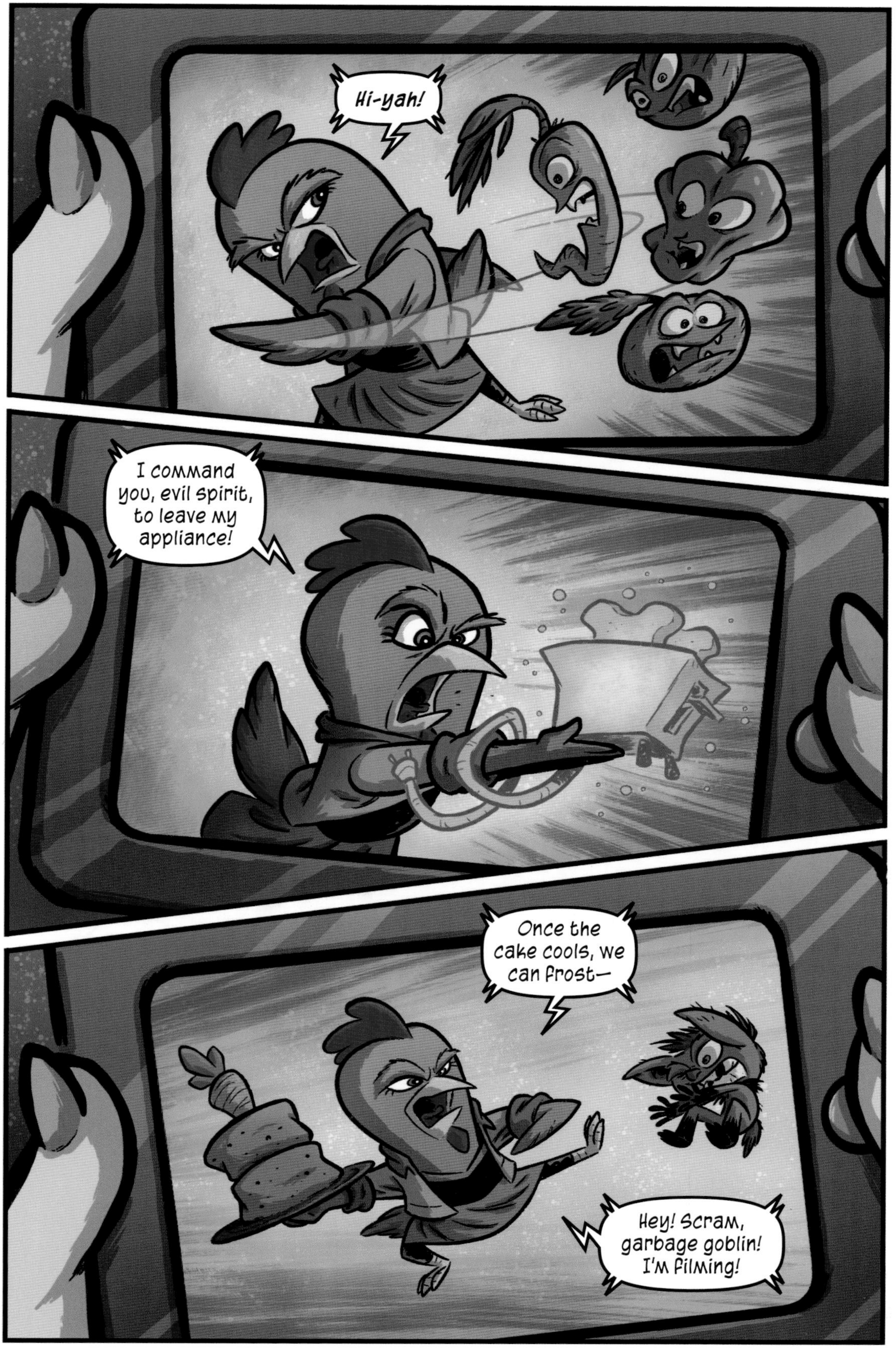
Hi-yah!
I command you, evil spirit, to leave my appliance!
Once the cake cools, we can frost—
Hey! Scram, garbage goblin! I'm filming!

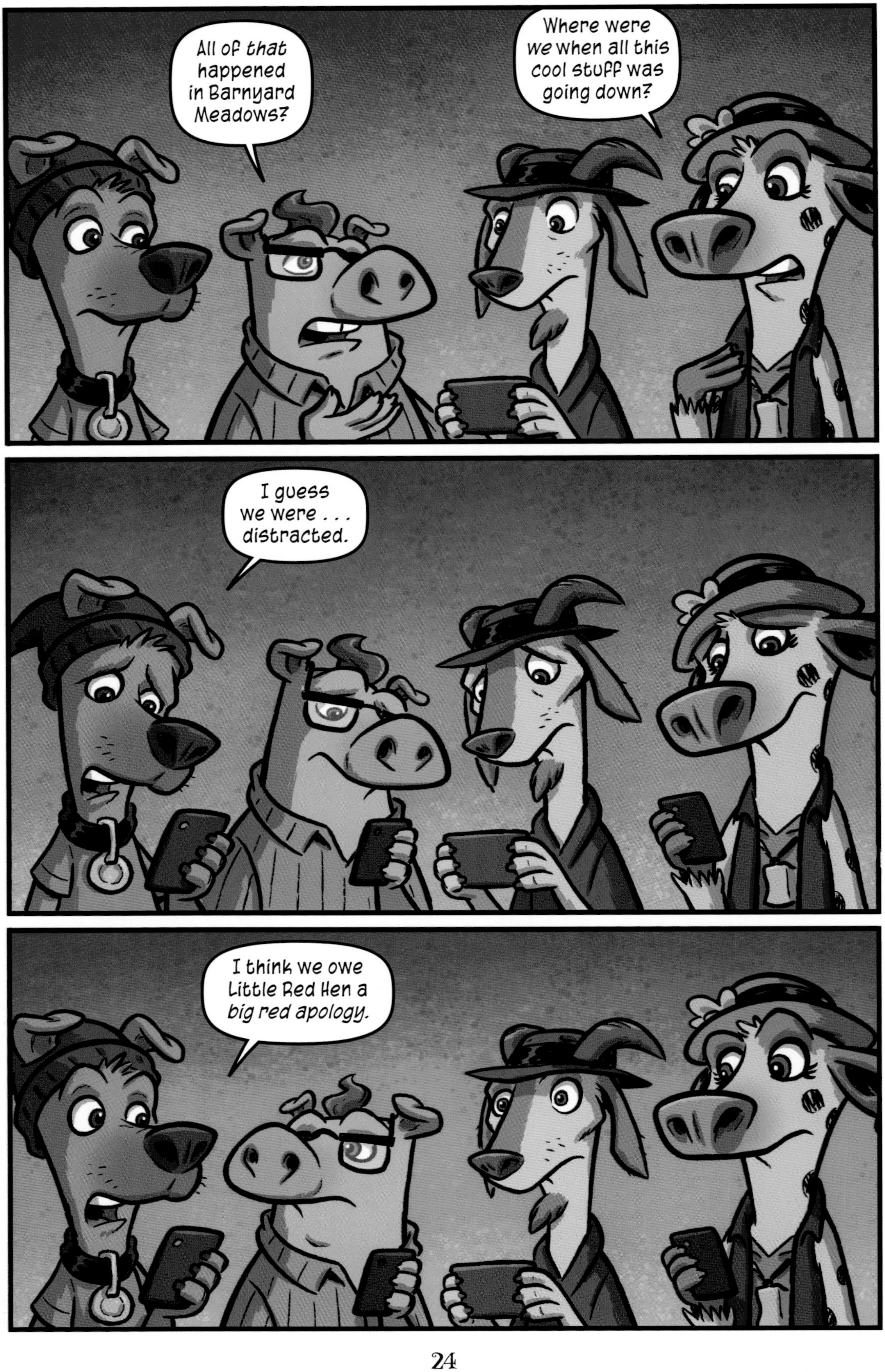
All of *that* happened in Barnyard Meadows?
Where were *we* when all this cool stuff was going down?
I guess we were . . . distracted.
I think we owe Little Red Hen a *big red apology.*

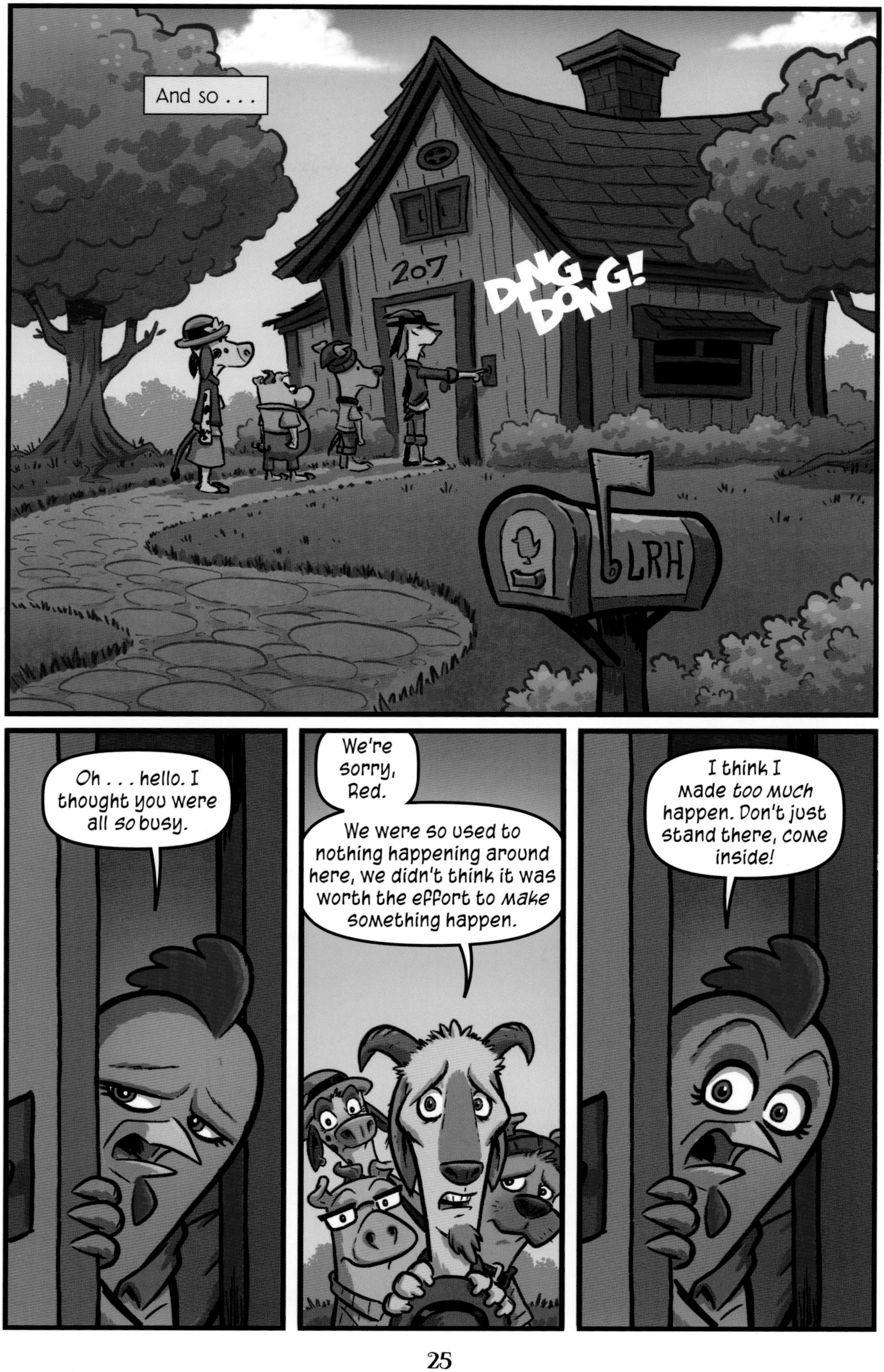
And so . . .
207
DING DONG!
LRH
Oh . . . hello. I thought you were all so busy.
We're sorry, Red.
We were so used to nothing happening around here, we didn't think it was worth the effort to make something happen.
I think I made too much happen. Don't just stand there, come inside!

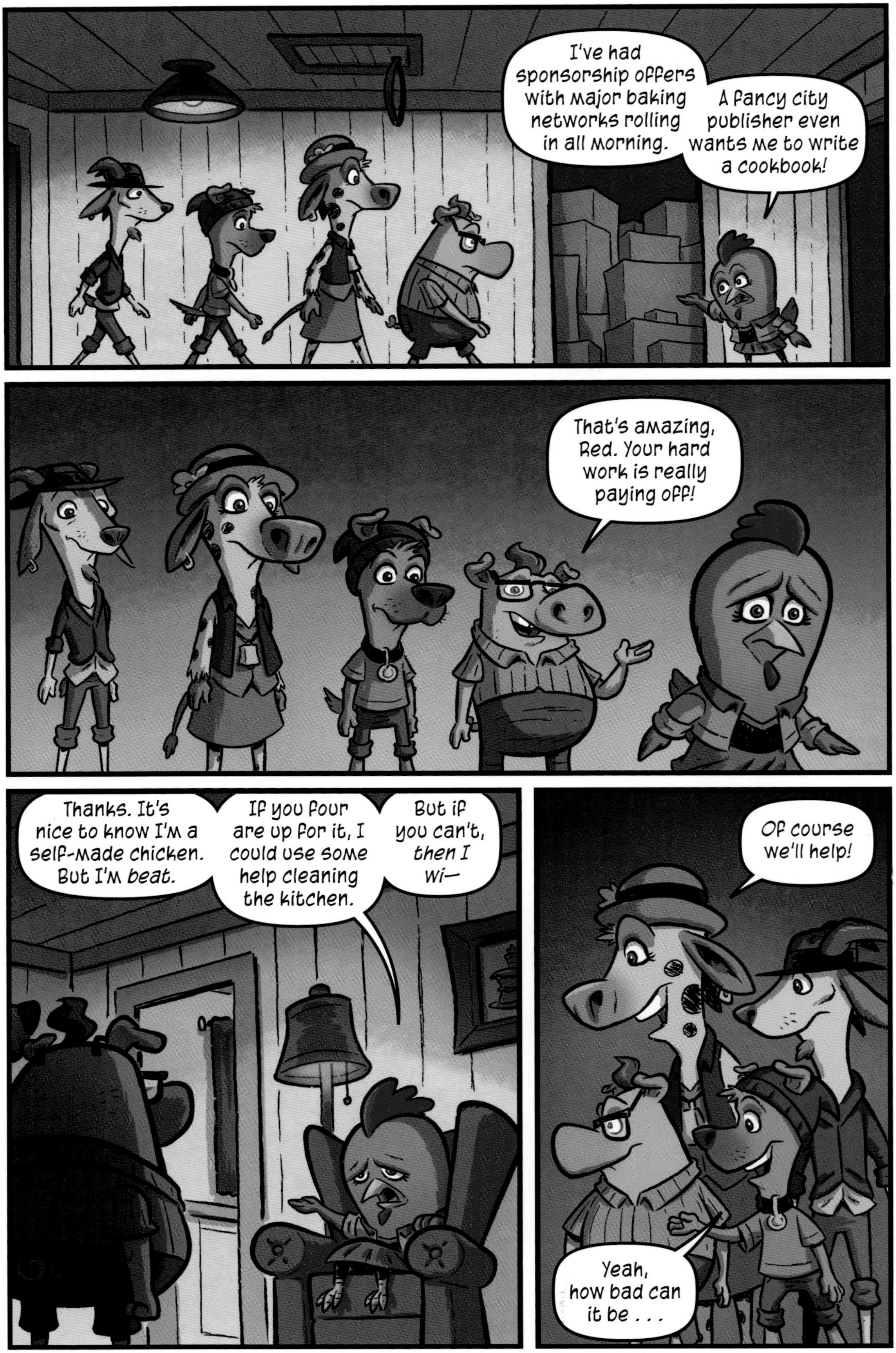
I've had sponsorship offers with major baking networks rolling in all morning.
A fancy city publisher even wants me to write a cookbook!
That's amazing, Red. Your hard work is really paying off!
Thanks. It's nice to know I'm a self-made chicken. But I'm *beat.*
If you four are up for it, I could use some help cleaning the kitchen.
But if you can't, *then I wi—*
Of course we'll help!
Yeah, how bad can it be . . .

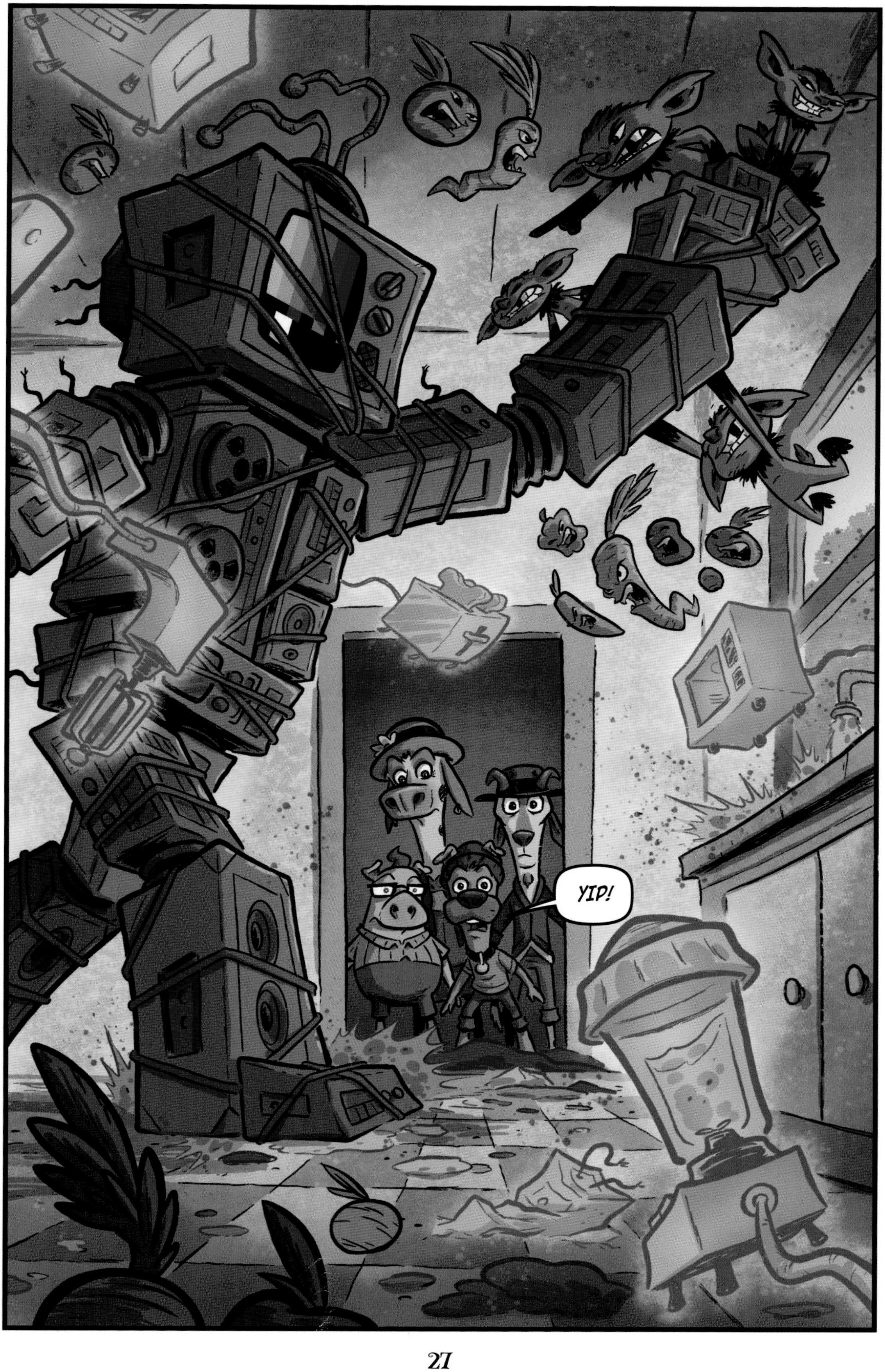
YIP!

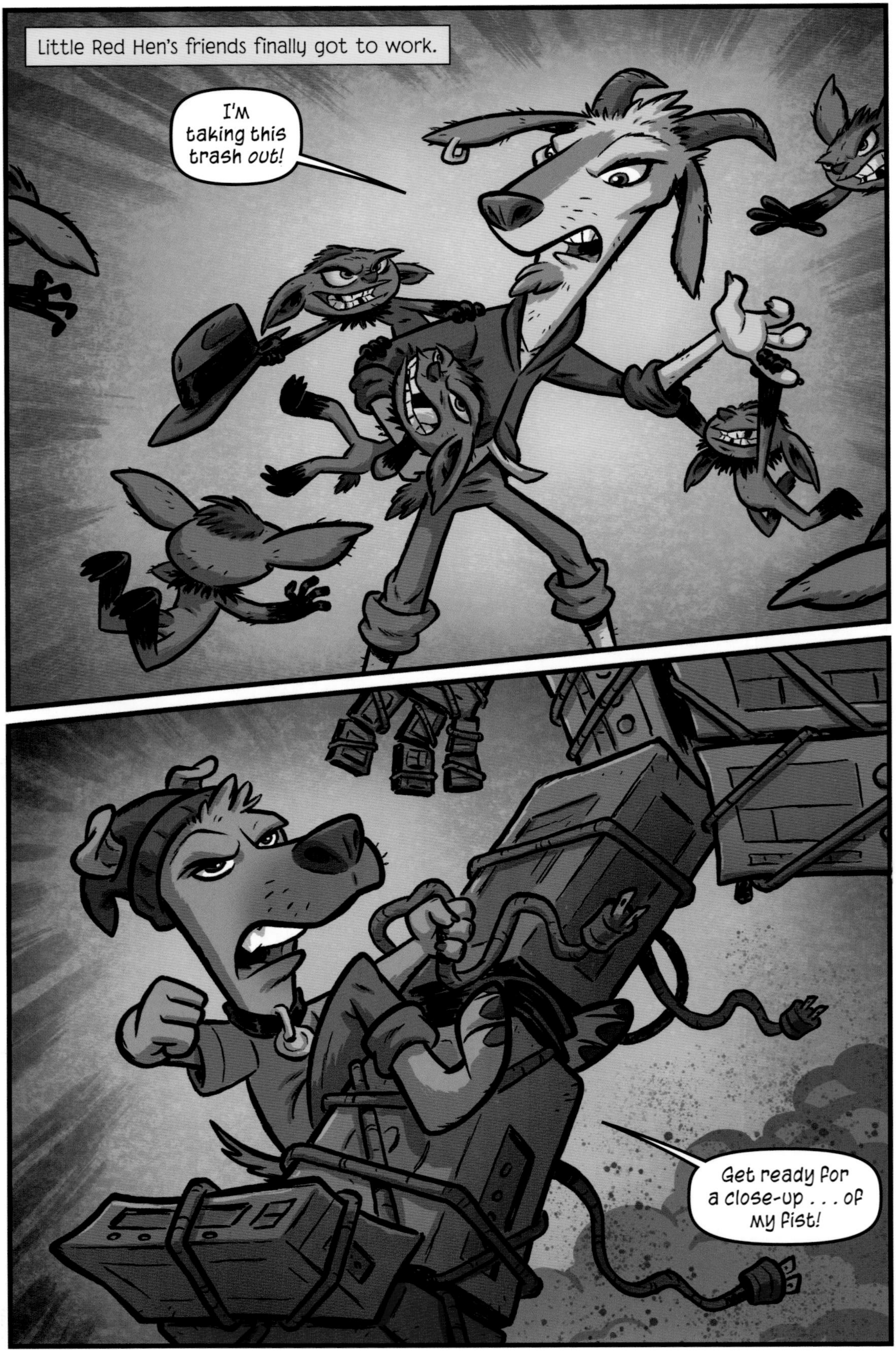
Little Red Hen's friends finally got to work.
I'M taking this trash out!
Get ready for a close-up . . . of my fist!

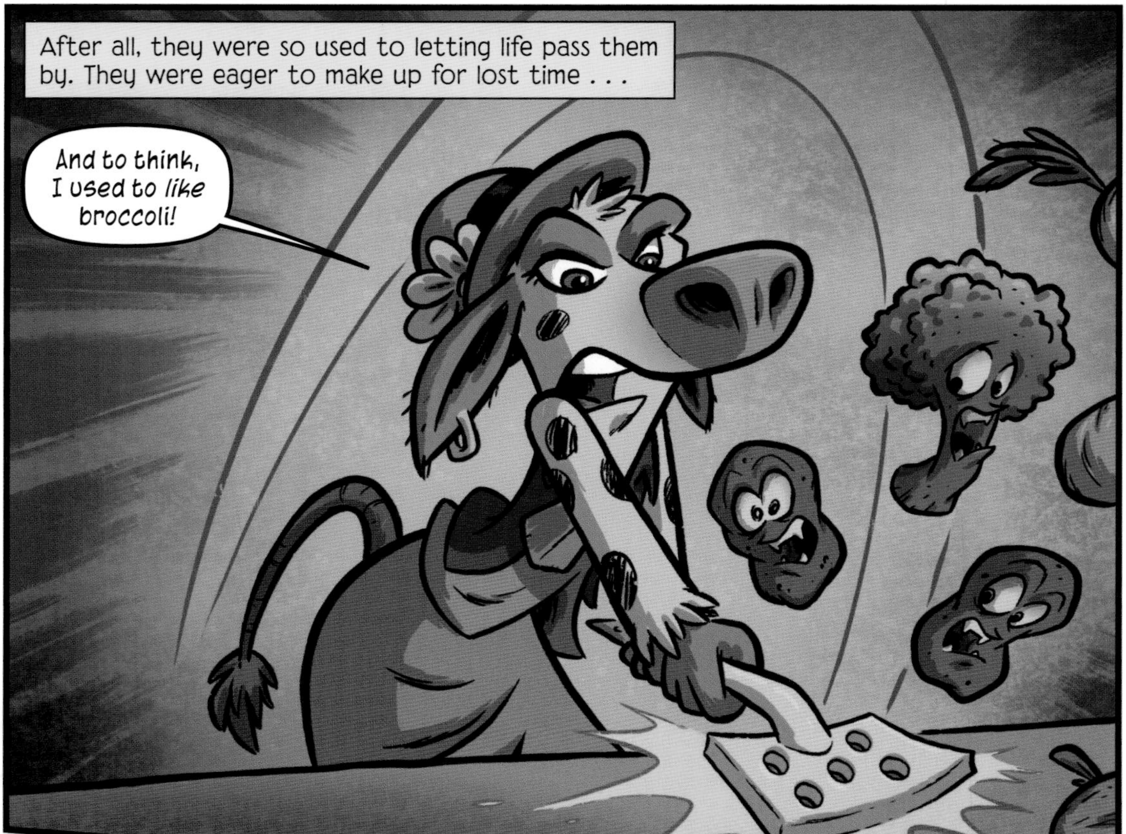
After all, they were so used to letting life pass them by. They were eager to make up for lost time . . .
And to think, I used to *like* broccoli!

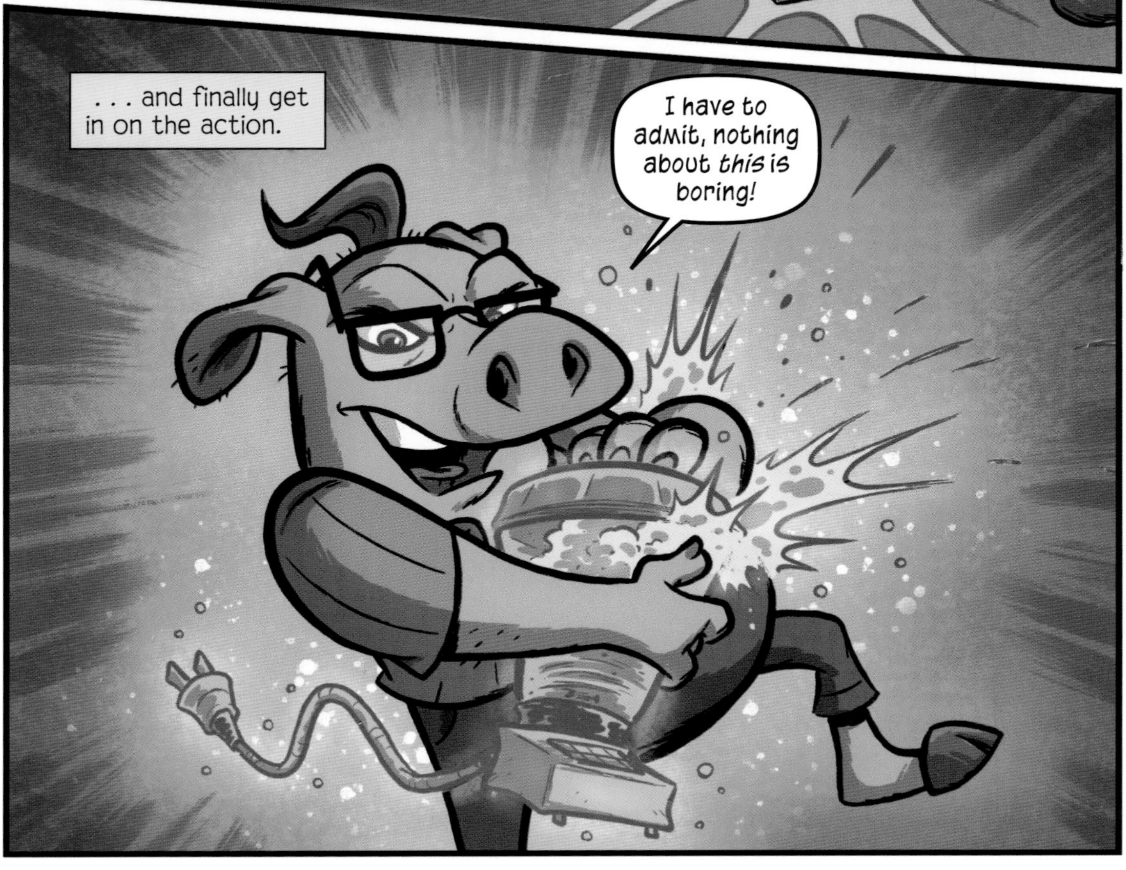
. . . and finally get in on the action.
I have to admit, nothing about *this* is boring!

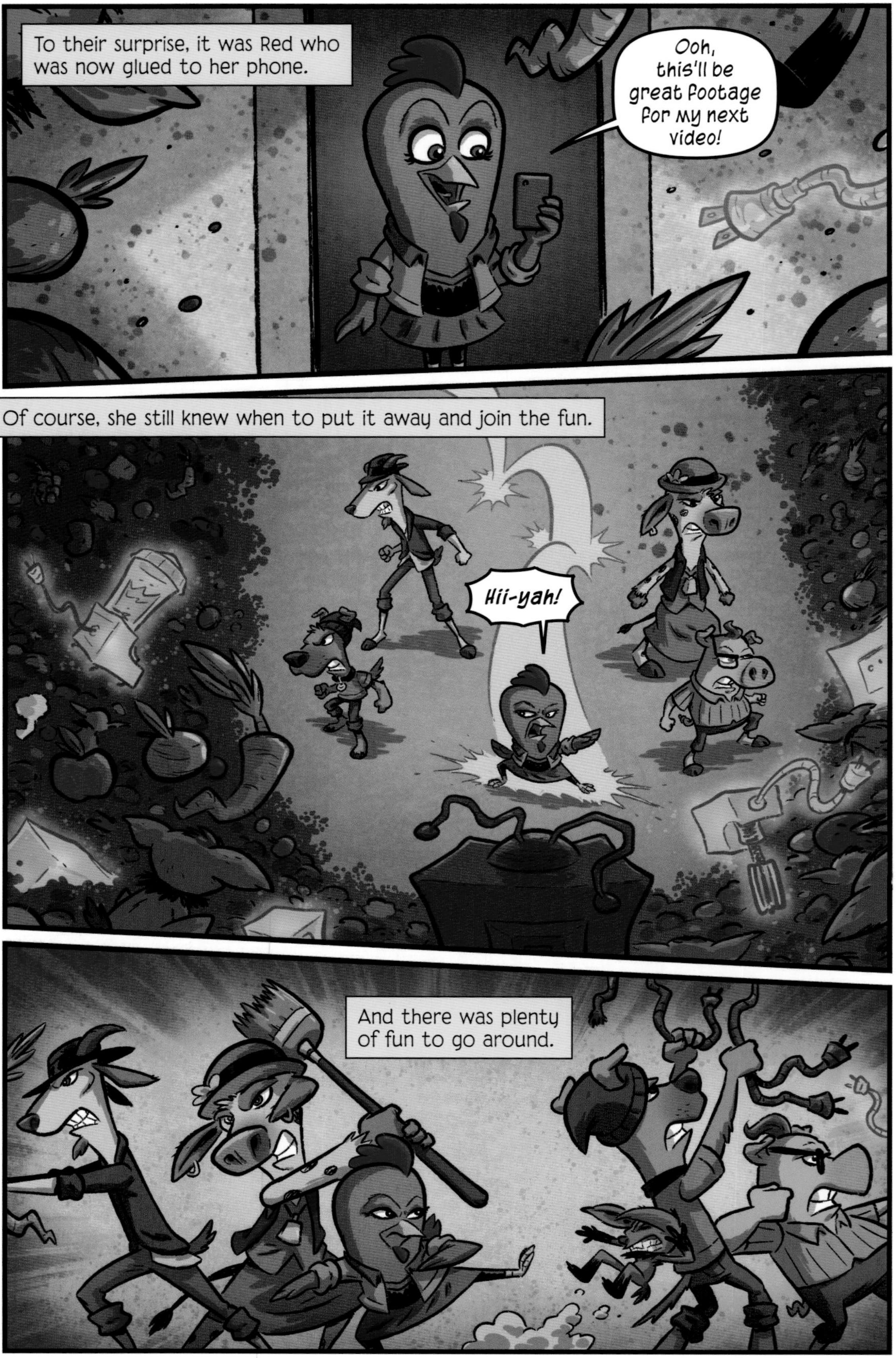
To their surprise, it was Red who was now glued to her phone.
Ooh, this'll be great footage for my next video!
Of course, she still knew when to put it away and join the fun.
Hii-yah!
And there was plenty of fun to go around.

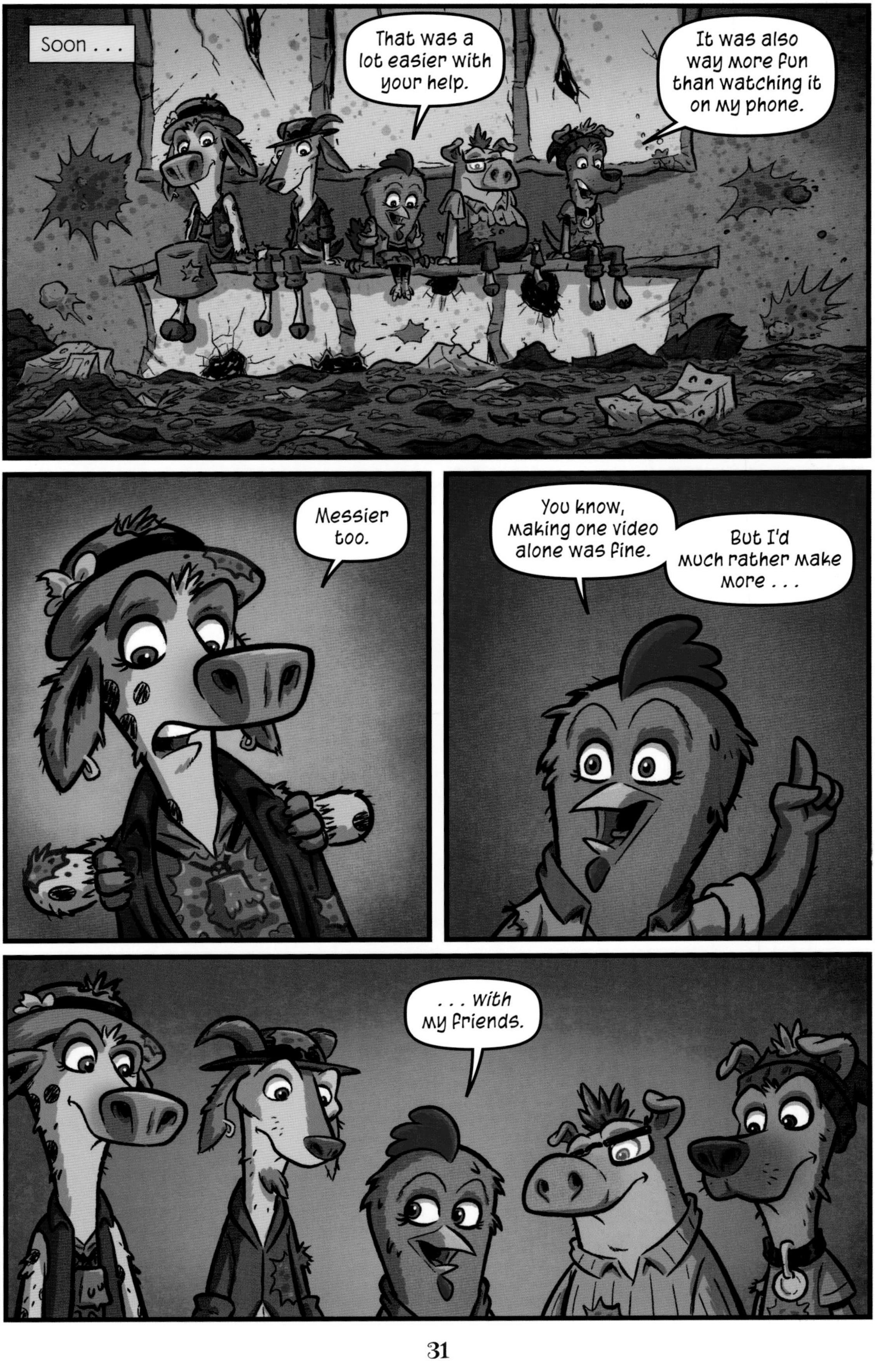
Soon . . .
That was a lot easier with your help.
It was also way more fun than watching it on my phone.
Messier too.
You know, making one video alone was fine.
But I'd much rather make more . . .
. . . with my friends.

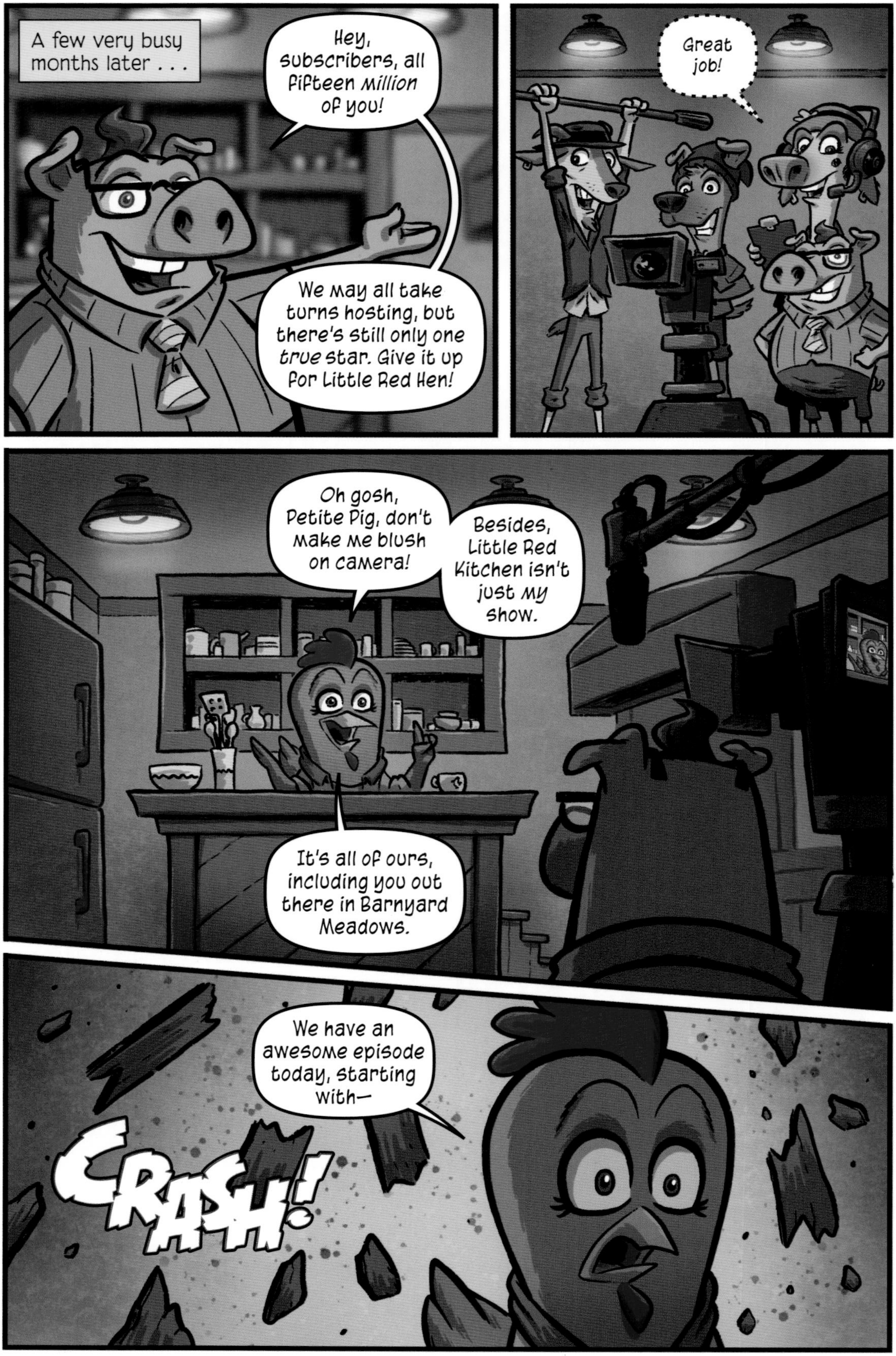
A few very busy months later . . .
Hey, subscribers, all fifteen *million* of you!
We may all take turns hosting, but there's still only one *true* star. Give it up for Little Red Hen!
Great job!
Oh gosh, Petite Pig, don't make me blush on camera!
Besides, Little Red Kitchen isn't just *my* show.
It's all of ours, including you out there in Barnyard Meadows.
We have an awesome episode today, starting with—
CRASH!

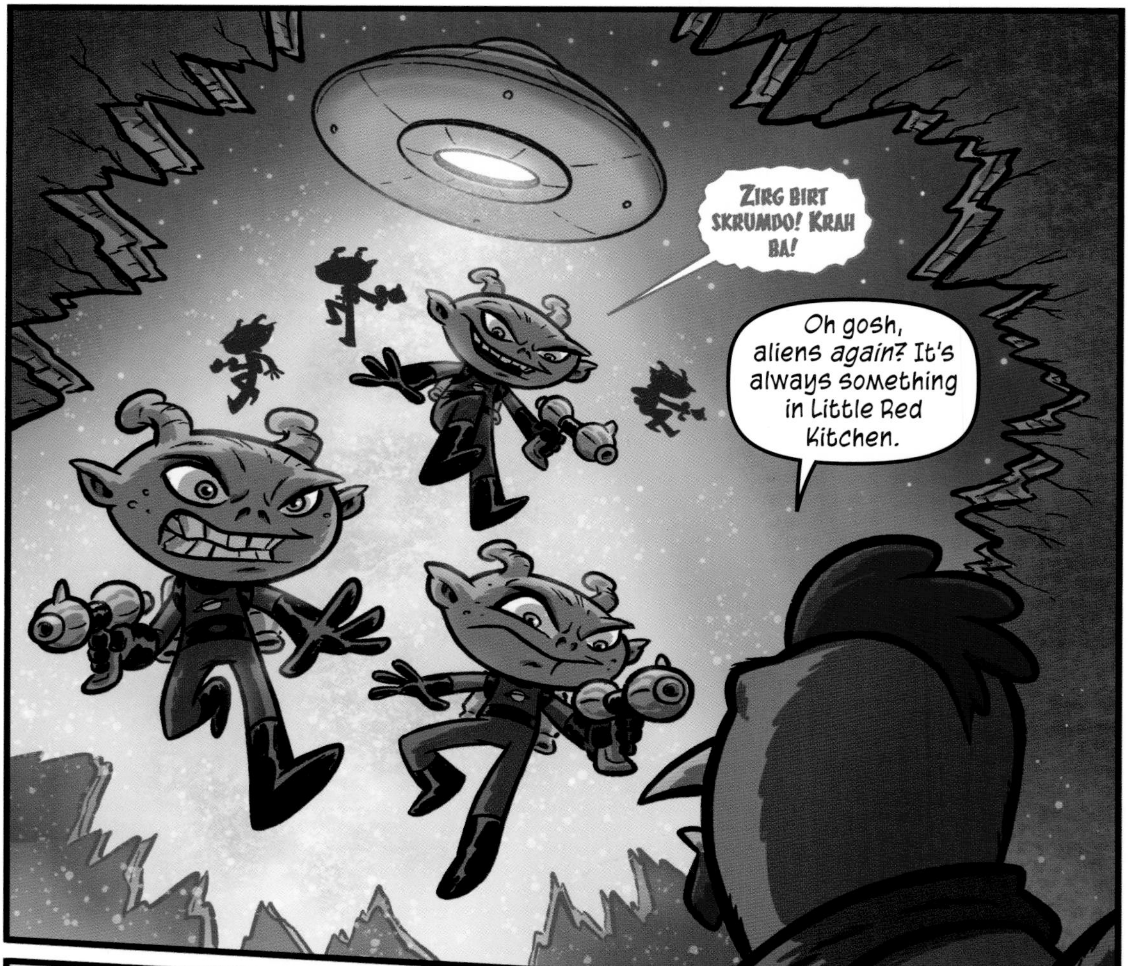
Zirg birt skrumdo! Krah ba!
Oh gosh, aliens *again*? It's always something in Little Red Kitchen.

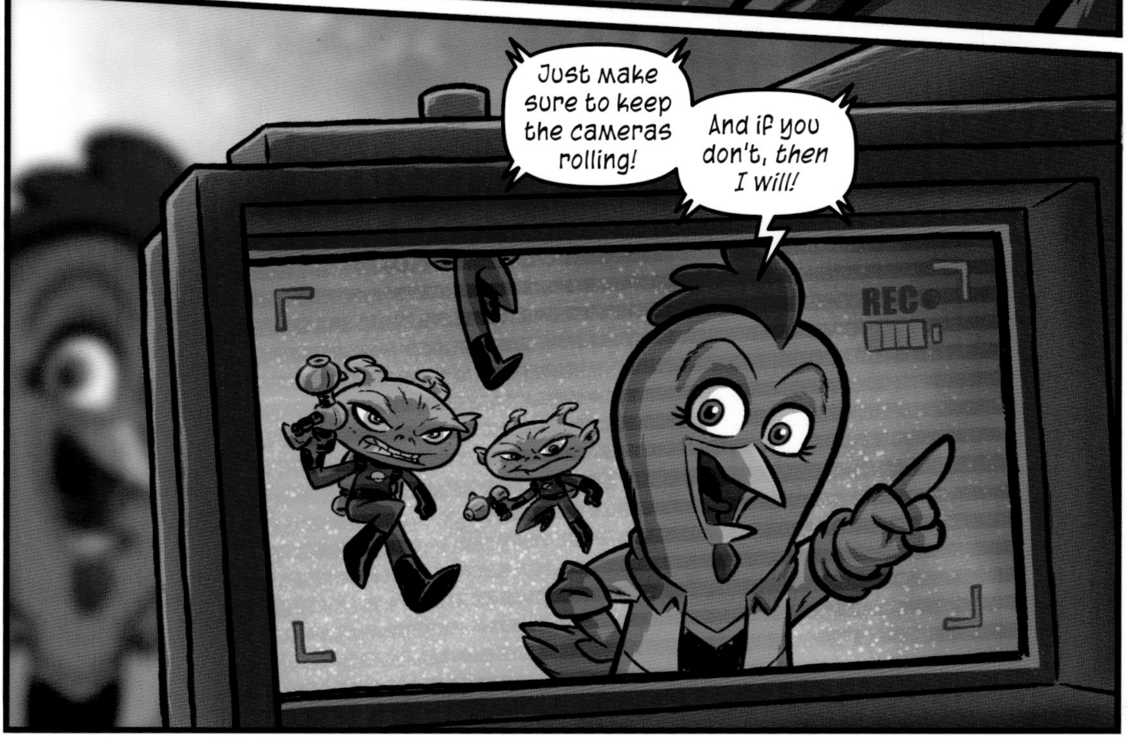
Just make sure to keep the cameras rolling!
And if you don't, *then* I will!
REC

ALL ABOUT FABLES

A fable is a short tale that teaches the reader a lesson about life, often with animal characters. At the end, there's almost always a moral (a fancy word for lesson) stated right out so you don't miss it. The story of a hardworking little red hen was first published by author Mary Mapes Dodge in 1874. She based it on an old folktale her mother used to tell her. Read on to learn more about the original fable and its moral. Can you spot any other lessons?

THE LITTLE RED HEN

One day, a little red hen comes across some wheat seeds. She decides to use them to bake bread. She goes around the farm asking other animals to help her plant the wheat, but all of the animals turn her down. At every step in the process, the little red hen asks her barnyard friends for help. And at every step in the process, the other animals turn her down. Eventually, the little red hen has planted, harvested, milled, and baked the wheat all on her own. When she finally has some fresh loaves of bread, she asks the other animals if they would like to help her eat the baked goods. This time, all the animals say yes, but the hen storms away in a huff. Since she had to make the bread all by herself, she's going to eat it all by herself too!

THE MORAL

NO WORK, NO PROFIT.
(In other words, don't expect others to do all the hard work. Help out!)

A FAR OUT GUIDE TO THE FABLE'S VIRAL TWISTS!

The original hen wants to plant, harvest, and bake wheat into bread. In this story, Little Red Hen wants to create a BarnTube baking channel.

The hen doesn't share any of her bread at the end of the classic tale. Red is a lot nicer and is thrilled when her friends join the channel!

This story isn't set on a regular farm. It takes place in Barnyard Meadows, which isn't as normal (or boring) as some might think!

In the original, the hen's only trouble is not having help. In the far out version, Red comes across garbage goblins, vampire veggies, robotic equipment, and haunted appliances!

VISUAL QUESTIONS

Why does this word balloon look different than others? Flip through the story and find more examples of unique balloons.

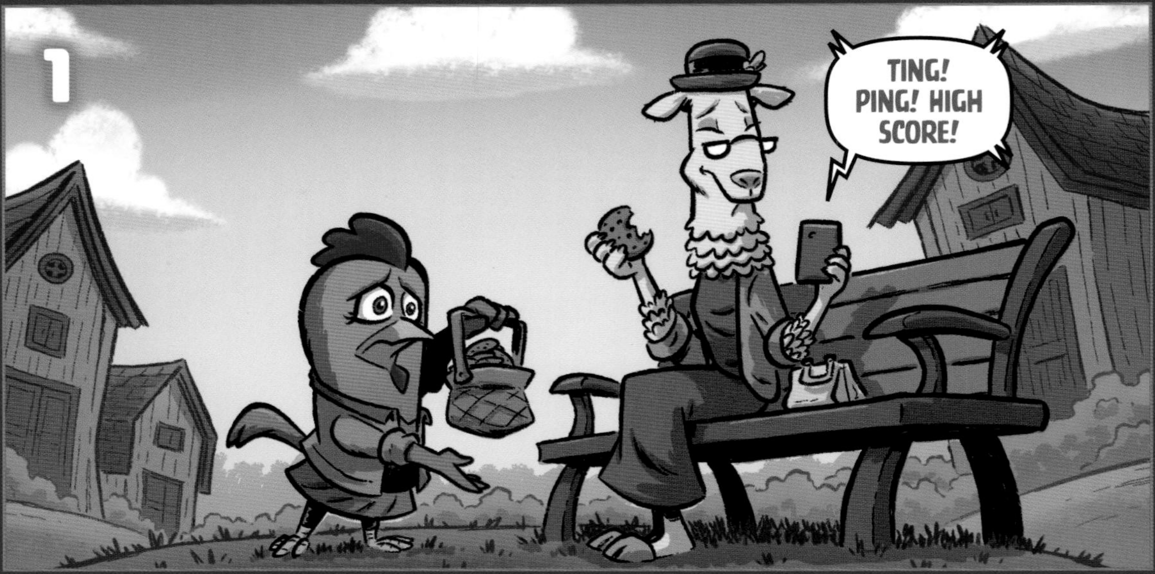
1
TING! PING! HIGH SCORE!

What is happening in the background of this panel on page 14? How does it hint at what's to come?

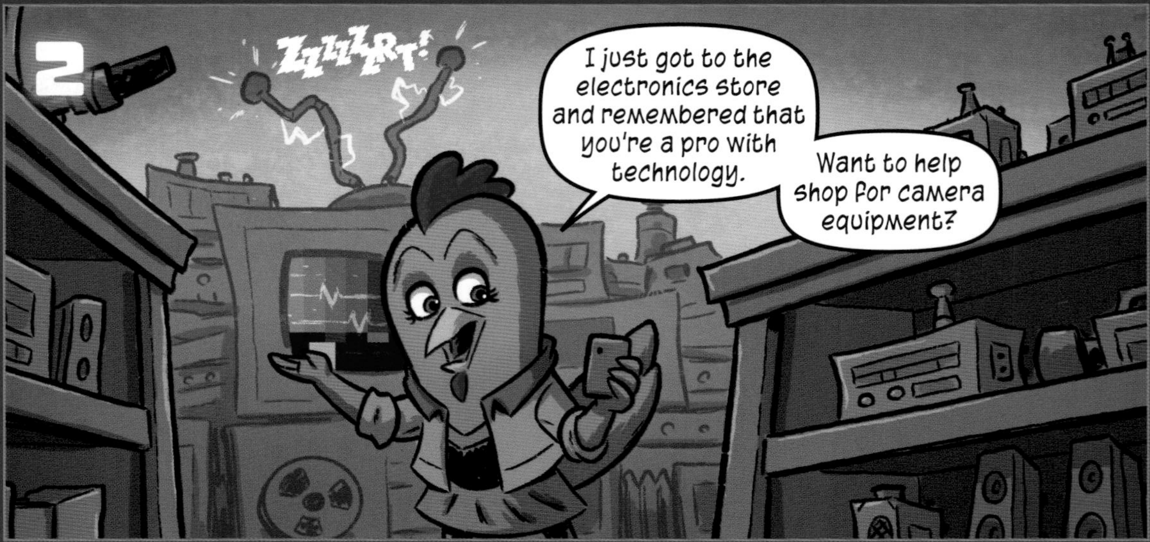
2
ZZZZZRT!
I just got to the electronics store and remembered that you're a pro with technology.
Want to help shop for camera equipment?

Describe how the friends feel here. How do their attitudes about helping Red change throughout the story?

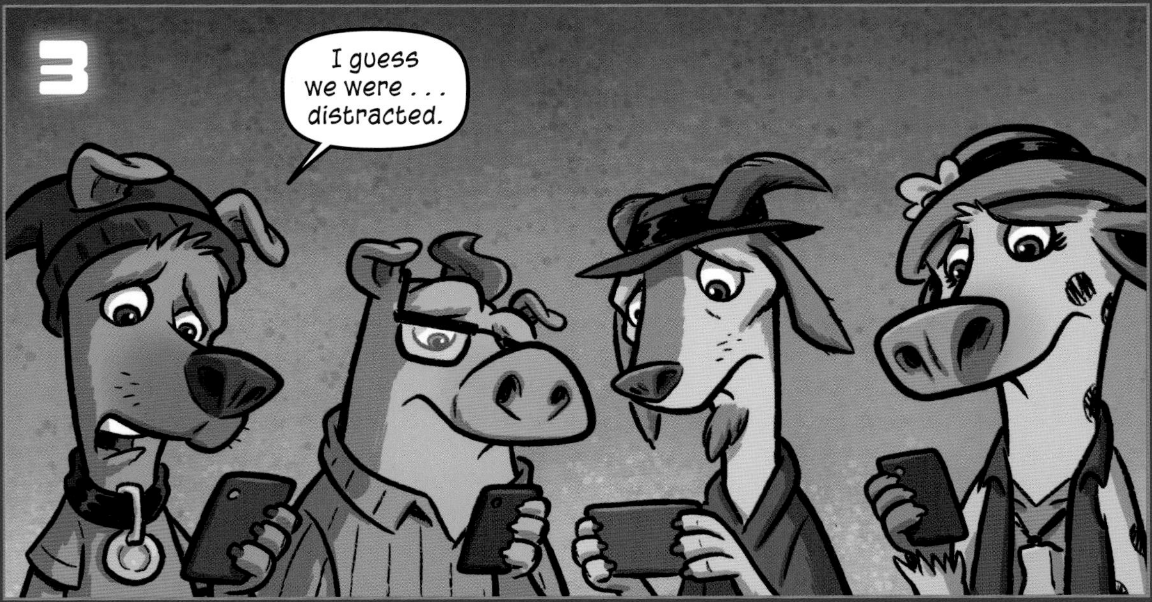
3
I guess we were . . . distracted.

Do you think Red liked working on the video by herself? Why or why not? Use examples from the text and art to back up your answer.

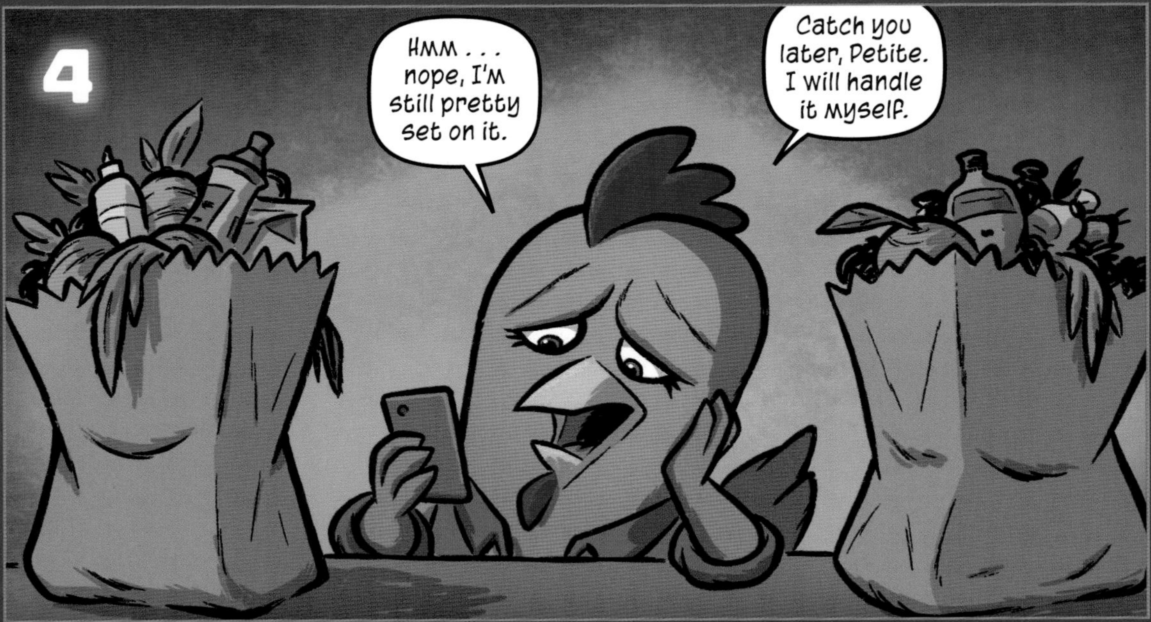
4
HMM . . . nope, I'M still pretty set on it.
Catch you later, Petite. I will handle it Myself.

AUTHOR

Steve Foxe is the author of more than 50 children's books and comics for properties including Pokémon, Batman, Transformers, Adventure Time, Steven Universe, and Grumpy Cat. He lives in Queens, New York. He's too lazy to start his own baking channel, but he does bake (and eat) plenty of bread, pastries, cookies, and brownies for fun.

ILLUSTRATOR

Otis Frampton is a comic book writer and illustrator. He is also one of the character and background artists on the popular animated web series How It Should Have Ended. His comic book series Oddly Normal is published by Image Comics.

GLOSSARY

appliance (uh-PLEYE-uhns)—a machine, such as an oven or microwave, that is used inside the house

attention span (uh-TEN-shuhn SPAN)—the amount of time you are able to think about something and stay interested in it

channel (CHA-nuhl)—an account on a website where you can post things such as videos and share them with others

discouraged (dih-SKUR-ijd)—feeling sad and feeling as if you will not be able to do something

distracted (dih-STRAK-tid)—unable to focus because your thoughts are on something else

equipment (ih-KWIP-muhnt)—all the things needed for a job or an activity

footage (FOO-tij)—action that has been recorded on video

host (HOST)—to lead a show and talk to guests who come on it

infestation (in-feh-STAY-shun)—when a large group of something has come into an area and is causing damage

sponsorship (SPON-sur-ship)—money given by a group that helps pay for an event or activity (or internet show!)

viral (VEYE-ruhl)—spreading quickly to many people, especially by being shared on the internet

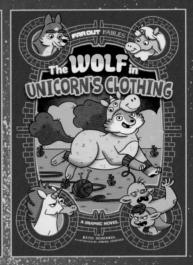
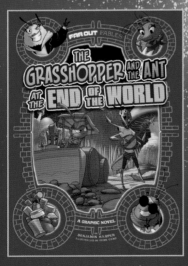